"*Star Trail*," Cole said, "keeping everything as best you can to scale, show the other locations of all the seeded ancient cultures."

Over six hundred green dots appeared forming a half moon. The sphere included numbers of them.

"Look where the Milky Way and all of our seeded galaxies are," Echo said.

Cole just stared at the screen.

The pattern was very, very clear.

The Milky Way was directly between the ancients' old home worlds and the half-moon of six hundred seeded cultures.

And now, for the first time, Cole understood why the ancients wouldn't tell anyone where their new home was.

They were afraid of something.

They were afraid of something in these cultures they had seeded.

Cole glanced at Echo. Her beautiful blue eyes were huge as she stared up at him.

"What the hell is going on here?" she whispered.

He just wished he had an answer for her.

STARBURST

ALSO BY DEAN WESLEY SMITH

THE SEEDERS UNIVERSE

Dust and Kisses: A Seeders Universe Prequel Novel

Against Time

Sector Justice

Morning Song

The High Edge

Star Mist

Star Rain

Star Fall

Starburst

Rescue Two

STARBURST

A SEEDERS UNIVERSE NOVEL

DEAN WESLEY SMITH

wmg
PUBLISHING

Starburst
Copyright © 2022 by Dean Wesley Smith
First published in *Smith's Monthly #37,* October 2016
Published by WMG Publishing
Cover and Layout copyright © 2022 by WMG Publishing
Cover art copyright © Philcold | Dreamstime
ISBN-13: 978-1-56146-733-4
ISBN-10: 1-56146-733-2

SECTION ONE

THE MISSION

PROLOGUE

E cho, can't you just relax a little?"

Echo glanced around at her best friend and lover, Cole Lemmon, as he followed her up the center of the deserted suburban street. The day was hot and Cole was sweating, staining his white T-shirt around the brown straps of the backpack he carried. His longish brown hair was damp where it stuck out from under his Yankee's baseball cap.

His handsome face was flushed even though they had only gone four blocks in distance.

She was hot as well, which was why she had been walking fast, trying to get them to their starting target before they stopped or the heat got them. It normally wasn't this hot in Portland, Oregon, or at least that's what some long-time residents of the area had told her earlier.

She was wearing jeans with tennis shoes, a sleeveless blue tank-top with a sports bra under it, and she had her short blonde hair under a Dodgers baseball cap. Sweat was running off her neck and down her chest and she desperately needed a drink of water.

She had her Smith and Wesscn pistol in a holster on her hip and Cole had a small twenty-two saddle rifle tied to the side of his backpack. It had been years since they had gone anywhere in this city without those guns, winter or summer. They both had admitted they would fee. naked without them, even though they could teleport away from any problem at an instant's notice.

But now, after three years mostly living on the surface of this planet, trying to help the residents recover from a horrid disaster, she and Cole had decided it was just easier to act like locals instead of Seeders. And locals all still carried guns, for the most part.

On both sides of the suburban street around them, the houses were like tombstones for the people who had been killed inside of them when the Big Death happened five years before. The once-green lawns where children had played were brown and had long turned to tall, dry weeds. The house windows were dirty and almost every house had drapes pulled, at least on the lower floors.

Weeds and grass had started growing in patches of dirt along the street and up through cracks in the concrete. What had been perfect lines of lawns, driveways, sidewalks, and street were now blurred as Mother Nature slowly took back the neighborhood.

Echo had seen a projection on how in fifty years a neighborhood like this would be completely overgrown, in one hundred years it would be all plants and piles of rubble, and in five hundred years it would be almost impossible to tell what had been here.

Just as Mother Nature had killed most everyone on the planet one day with a burst of electromagnetic waves from space, she now was slowly reclaiming the planet.

The Big Death had hit at a little after eight in the morning here in Portland, so most people in this neighborhood were either at work or taking kids to school or some such thing.

Cole and Echo had come to this planet as part of the Seeders reconstruction program. They had been a couple for almost fifty years. Cole was just over two hundred years old while Echo had just gone past one hundred. One of the wonderful things about being a Seeder was that you never aged.

But she was sure that this task, being on this planet, was aging them both. She knew, without a doubt, that no matter how long they lived or how many planets they visited, they would never forget this.

Seeing death every day and living in the middle of it did that to a person.

They lived together in the city of Portland, Oregon, worked together both on the local newspaper, and searching for the dead, and she couldn't imagine being without Cole through any of it.

They also had a nice apartment on their base Seeder ship, *Silver Moon*, but these days they seldom jumped back to that place. Here in Portland they had adopted two wonderful cats and she actually liked the home better here with the cats. When they left this assignment, she planned on taking the cats with them.

She looked around at all the empty houses. This neighbor-

5

hood hadn't been cleared yet, which was the process they were sent to start.

They were to inventory the bodies in every home along the street and mark from the outside which homes had bodies so the removal crews could come and take the bodies to the new cemeteries.

And in each home she and Cole were to look for information as to who lived there and double-check it with their database, even those houses without bodies.

The ultimate goal of the Respect Project was to give everyone who died in the Big Death a proper resting place and a record of their existence for the future, including where they had lived and what they had done for work.

It was almost an impossible task, but everyone in the five now-growing new cities around the country, which included Portland, and the new national government, were committed to the task.

Both Cole and Echo thought it a wonderful task and worth every minute they spent doing it. It would be part of the rebuilding of the civilization on this planet.

"We can start anywhere, you know?" Cole said. "How about we start here, work back to the truck along both sides, then cool down and bring the truck to here and go the other direction?"

Echo stopped and glanced at an address still visible on the side of one of the homes. From what she could tell, they were about halfway along the long subdivision street. Cole's idea was a good one. They had to get out of the sun. It was only ten in the morning and this day promised to be far too hot to stay out in the sun for very long.

She nodded. "Good plan."

"Thank you," Cole said, stopping and taking off his pack, letting it drop to the concrete in the middle of the street.

They had been going out four mornings a week to catalog houses and bodies in the vast subdivisions that surrounded Portland. It had bothered her some at first, nosing into people's personal homes, but then she had grown numb to it. After all, the people they were investigating were all dead.

The thing she could never look at were the children's bodies, often in cribs. Every time they found a home with a child, Cole took that house on his own, even though they had clear orders to always stay together. Not that there was anything dangerous in these old subdivisions besides slowly rotting wood.

This subdivision had lots of signs that children lived in these homes, from swing sets visible in the backyards, to small bikes and other toys left near the front doors.

She really never wanted children and Seeders seldom had children, actually. Cole had no desire for children either. But that didn't mean she could stomach seeing a dead child. There were some things she would draw the line at.

Period.

She took a long drink of semi-cold water that tasted wonderful and then handed the bottle to Cole, who took a drink and sighed. Around them a slight breeze kicked up filling the air with faint noises of houses creaking and dry brush rustling. The sounds did nothing to break the death silence of the subdivision.

"Let's go get snoopy into people's lives," he said, handing her back the bottle of water.

"That one first," she said, pointing to a light blue house on her right. "Let's do two on that side, then two on the other side, as we work back to the truck."

"Sounds perfect," he said, smiling at her and picking up his pack.

She loved everything about him, his dark eyes, his solid build, and his strong arms. But mostly she just loved that smile.

Somehow, over all the years of living now in the middle of death, that smile of his had kept her sane.

They headed up the front sidewalk of the two-story home that must have been very nice in its day for this time in this planet's history. The drapes were pulled and more than likely the front door was locked. Both of them had been trained before they started this job to pick a lock. Cole was slightly faster at it than she was, but only by a second or so. They hadn't found a lock so far that had stopped them.

The people in charge of the Respect Project wanted all the homes to be respected, if possible, even though eventually they would all just rot away. Echo was fine with that as well.

Cole left his pack on the front step and took out his rifle, slinging it over his shoulder before bending down and picking the front door locks. Thirty seconds later he stood and pushed the door open.

The smell of mold and dust and something with a slight tang greeted them and they both stepped back out of the smell and pulled out their cloth masks and tied them over their mouths and noses. That smell with a bite meant there was a body in the building.

They always wore masks when a body was in the building.

The masks also helped them with the dust. They went

through about a dozen of the masks a day, maybe more on a hot day like today.

Even though there was some light filtering through the drapes and from a back window in the kitchen beyond the living room, they both clicked on flashlights. When they first started out doing this job, they had both tripped over various things in homes that they just hadn't seen in dim light. So they took no chances now.

Echo panned her flashlight around the living room. More of a formal room that didn't look much used. A layer of gray dust dulled down all colors in the room.

Moving slowly to not kick up too much dust from five years of no one moving around in here, they headed for the kitchen and the family room beyond.

Echo was relieved to see no sign of children's toys around the family room.

Cole slowly opened some drawers near the family dining area. Often families left personal information in drawers near a kitchen table.

While he was doing that, she turned and opened the back door leading into a two-car garage. There was one car there. And a spot for a second one. Tools were in their places on the walls.

Nothing else of interest.

"One car left," she said as she went past Cole and toward the rooms to the right of the big living room. One looked like a guest bedroom and was as sterile as the living room. Whoever lived in this house believed in keeping everything in its place. Even after sitting abandoned for five years and layers of gray dust making everything pale, that feeling of "in its place" was clear in this home.

It made her wonder what the residents of this home had been like. Clearly different than her and Cole. Their large apartment in a building in the downtown area was always awash with clutter of various types, mostly books. They were both just comfortable in that.

And their apartment on board *Silver Moon* was the same way. Cluttered and comfortable.

She would not have been comfortable in this place. It felt sterile and even more dead than most homes she had been in, as if this home had been dead before the Big Death hit.

"Anything?" she asked.

Cole shook his head. "Nothing. Drawers in perfect order, but no bills, no letters, nothing. More than likely all that is in a study someplace from the looks of all this."

With Cole leading, they headed upstairs.

The light was brighter upstairs as most of the back windows in the home had the blinds open. They all looked out over a lush backyard that had held a pool. Echo had no doubt it had been beautiful in its day. And from the looks of the house, the lawn would have been mowed perfectly and the pool more than likely cleaned twice a week.

At the top of the stairs a hallway lead the length of the house. It had a number of closed doors. Echo had a hunch behind one of those doors would be the body they knew was in here from the faint musty smell. The smell had a slight tang to it after five years, but it wasn't a smell that was easy to miss.

And now that they were upstairs, the smell was thick.

And even though it was still fairly early, this upper area of the house was already heating up. Any body they did find would be well mummified in this kind of heat.

A mummified body was a lot better as far as Echo was concerned than a body torn up from animals. Not all animals had survived the electromagnetic pulse. Dogs and rats and mice had been killed, but cats had survived. And with a cat trapped in a home with a dead human, they ate the dead human when they got hungry enough.

There were no signs this home had cats, so the body would be mummified and look moderately human even after five years.

The first two doors were to small bedrooms with no occupants. The rooms had been furnished with small single beds and just left. One room was painted pink, one blue.

Clearly the rooms had been meant for future children that had not arrived yet.

And now never would.

The third door was to an empty bathroom and the next door was to a master bedroom and bath, also empty. The bed was made perfectly.

There was nothing out of place in this entire house. Echo found that amazing and very closed up and creepy.

The next door on the other side of the hall was to a study with a big desk.

"Got it," Cole said, moving to the desk and file cabinet that would let them know who had lived here.

There was one more door at the end of the hall and that meant it had the body in it.

Echo went to it and opened it slowly, making sure to not stir up any dust as she did so.

The blinds were open in the room and it was a fairly large family room that also did not look used in any way. This room had a large screen television, a number of couches, a game table, and plush carpet.

It had been designed to be comfortable, but clearly not made comfortable.

Everything again was in perfect position. Nothing was used. It was as if the people living in this house had just existed in it and never really lived in it.

There was a door off the family room that was closed. More than likely that was where the body was. They had found many bodies, since they started this job, in various stages of bathroom routines.

Cole came in behind her. "This is the home of Ben and Cathy Freeman. He worked at a pharmacy downtown and she was an RN."

Cole held up his digital pad. "We already recovered his body when they cleaned the downtown area."

"This place sure looks like they were planning for kids," Echo said. "Clearly didn't get the chance."

Cole glanced around and nodded. Then he pointed to the door. "You want me to look and see who is in there?"

"We both will," she said.

Slowly she opened the bathroom door to keep the dust from swirling while both of them shined their flashlights into the small bathroom.

What she saw stunned her and took her a moment for her mind to wrap around.

What had been a fairly attractive, thin, brown-haired woman lay in the bathtub face up. She had mummified, but she still looked pretty good, with her long brown hair fanned out on the back of the tub over her.

And her face was calm in death. Very calm.

What had really surprised Echo was that the tub water when it evaporated had left an ugly brown stain.

It took her a moment to see why. Both of the woman's wrists that were crossed over her chest had been slashed.

A razor blade lay on a napkin on the edge of the tub.

"Now that's a first," Cole said beside Echo in the bathroom door. "More than likely she cut her wrists right before the Big Death hit."

On the counter was a note card standing up with the name "Ben" on it.

Echo looked at it, then glanced at Cole. Clearly that was Cathy Freeman's suicide note.

Cole shrugged, meaning she could read it or not. Up to her.

Echo wasn't sure if she wanted to read it, but at this point she felt she had no choice.

She picked up the note and opened it. Then read it aloud as Cole held his flashlight so she could see.

Dearest Ben,

I am so sorry for the mess I have left you. I have tried to keep this clean and simple and plan this in a bathroom we seldom use.

I am so sorry that I cannot bring the children into the world we so hoped to have. I could no longer look at the deadness in your eyes and the disappointment I felt every time we made love. My passing here will allow you to move on, to find a new wife, to be happy, and finally have and raise the children you so wanted.

Please don't be mad at me, love. This is for the best. Remember me to your children when they are old enough to understand. Have a wonderful life.

Love Always,
Cath

Echo carefully replaced the suicide note on the counter.

"Let's get out of here," Cole said, gently touching her elbow. "We got all we need from here."

Somehow Echo nodded and turned and followed Cole out of the family room and down the hall past the future children's bedrooms, then down the stairs and out into the hot air of the dead subdivision.

Cole marked the house, picked up his pack, stuck his rifle back in it, and led the way to the street.

She pulled off her mask and tucked it in her pocket, letting the warm air work to clear her mind.

They stopped in the middle of the street, both with their backs to the house they had just been in.

After a moment, Cole gently touched her arm. "You all right?"

"Honestly," she said, turning to look into his worried dark-blue eyes. "I think I'm done for the day."

"I agree," Cole said. "Too hot anyway. So what are you thinking?"

She looked into the eyes of the man she loved, the man that had helped her survive more death than she ever wanted to think about. "I am thinking about a long cold shower in our air-conditioned apartment."

"We are on the same track with that," Cole said, smiling.

"Then maybe a few hours in bed making love to you."

At that, his eyebrows went up and he looked at her, clearly puzzled.

"After all this death," she said, sweeping her arm around to indicate the dead neighborhood, "I just want to feel close to you, to be alive."

He smiled bigger than she had remembered him smiling in a very long time. "Perfect, just perfect."

She kissed him, then took his arm and together they headed up the hot street of the dead subdivision.

It would be a day she would never forget.

And this assignment on this mostly dead planet would also never be forgotten. No matter how long she lived.

CHAPTER 1
OVER 400 YEARS LATER

hairman Cole Lemmon stood next to the big command chair on the Starburst exploration ship *Star Trail*, leaning against the wide rail that separated the lower level from the next level of command.

He wore his normal jeans, dress shirt with the sleeves rolled up, and running shoes. He had on a blue ball cap with the brim pushed back off his forehead. He sipped on his normal morning cup of coffee, black and strong, as he watched the stream of data flowing over the massive screen in front of him.

He had longish brown hair, a square face, and looked to be in shape, with wide shoulders and a smile people said could calm an entire room.

In front of him, the main screen in the command center filled an entire thirty-foot-high wall and was twice that wide. At the moment, the wall was covered by flowing reports from the thousands of scout ships ahead of *Star Trail*, doing surveys of galaxies, two ships per galaxy.

He had watched these reports now every morning for over fifty years, since *Star Trail* had launched from the Milky Way galaxy. He never grew tired of it because he knew that at some point one of those scout ships would find something very special in one of those galaxies.

Maybe even a growing alien race, which excited him more than he wanted to think about.

Behind him in the command center, thirty of the best people he and his life partner, Echo, could find were at their stations. They were the main command crew. The command center was always manned with three different shifts covering different times of the day.

The command center was the beating heart of *Star Trail*.

The massive room was built like a large amphitheater. The chairmen's command chair, actually two chairs molded together, was on the lower level. Two steps up behind the command chair and the wide railing were four stations, with their second in command, JP Horshaw, to the right.

The next level up had eight stations and the level around the back wall and top had another eighteen stations. At this time of the day, with all the reports flowing in from all the scout ships exploring galaxies, all stations were occupied.

Everyone was busy, each with a specific task of not only keeping *Star Trail* and the three million souls on board safe, but studying in detail every report flowing in from the scout ships.

This was part of his morning ritual. He flat loved it. And the strong, black coffee in his mug.

Echo, his co-chairman, liked to exercise first thing in the morning, something he couldn't imagine doing. They were both runners and he liked to run later in the day, usually through some of the thousands of parks and forests covering millions and millions of square kilometers inside the ship.

There was one thing good about their conflicting exercise schedules. One of them was always in the command center during most of the day. They did each lunch and dinner together every day. They got a lot planned over those meals.

And they made sure they had time together every evening, even if to just sit and read.

With over three million Seeders on board, at first he had felt the responsibility of all those people more than he wanted to admit. Now he understood it.

He still felt it, but he understood it as well, which helped.

Star Trail was shaped like a giant bird soaring through space, with a pointed nose and wings frozen in place. It was so massive that every year the crew had a ten-person relay race that covered the nine thousand kilometer distance from the tip of the ship to the tail and then back to the tip. Every Starburst ship had the same relay. It had become a tradition for all of them.

Cole loved running in it because he saw parts of his own ship he would never have a chance to visit personally. His favorite run now was through the massive forests that covered millions of square kilometers. It made him feel for just a time that he wasn't inside a space ship.

"Chairman," Star Trail said, "Incoming message from Star Fall to all Starburst ships. Priority One."

Star Trail's voice was feminine and precise while remaining warm. He liked the voice a great deal. And when in the command chair it felt like *Star Trail* and he and Echo were almost one at times, the wonderful aspect of being chairmen of a Starburst ship.

"Have Chairman Guinn report to the command center at once."

A moment later Echo appeared at his side. Her short blonde hair was matted to her head in sweat and she had a towel over her shoulder that she was using to wipe off sweat from her face. She must have been in the last part of her exercise routine. She liked to do sprints. Another reason they seldom ran together.

To Cole she looked as beautiful today as the day they had met all those hundreds of years ago. She was about five-four, with a thin build that didn't really show how strong she was. She had dark blue eyes like his that could be both warm and harsh.

He never tired of looking into those eyes.

"What's happening?" she asked as she finished wiping sweat from her face and neck and let the towel drape over her shoulder.

He shrugged. "Priority one message from *Star Fall*. *Star Trail*, please put *Star Fall* through on the big screen when they are ready."

Around them the command center fell silent as everyone listened and watched.

Star Fall was another Starburst ship that had left the Milky Way at about the same time as they had. *Star Fall* had been one of the three ships to lead the successful war against a run-away genetic experiment that threatened all of the human space. Cole and Echo had only gotten involved in that war toward the end as the chairmen of *Star Trail*.

After the war, the Starburst program of sending out fourteen massive ships to explore in all directions through known space started. *Star Trail's* intelligence and personality was moved into the new, far larger ship they were in now.

The Starburst program had really shown benefits no one would have expected. In the last year or so, *Star Fall* had discovered the abandoned home of all humanity and Seeders, something no one even knew had existed. The massive area of space had also been the home of the two other intelligent races in known space, the Gray and the Cirrata.

Cole and Echo and all the other Starburst ships and crews had watched the unfolding story of exploring the old abandoned worlds and then finally meeting the ancients who had stayed behind in the old home center.

So now, with *Star Fall* contacting them and all the other Starburst ships, there was no telling what was happening. But Cole had a hunch it would be exciting.

On the big screen in front of Cole and Echo the familiar faces of four people appeared. The couple on the right and slightly back were Chairmen Matt and Carey of *Star Fall*. Both had wide smiles and seemed very much relaxed, which made Cole instantly drop one level of worry.

The two that faced the screen head on were Chairmen Ray and Tacita. They were over four million years old and before the discovery of the ancients, Ray and Tacita were thought to be the oldest Seeders alive. They had been the chairmen of the very first Seeders' mother ship to ever start to seed humanity in another galaxy.

Turns out they had also been seeded by the ancients and helped along for a period of time.

21

Cole and Echo sort of thought of them as grandparents, even though both looked not much older than any other Seeder. Tacita had short, black hair and eyes that seemed to cut through a person and Ray wore his gray hair long and down his back.

Cole had no idea how anyone could live four million years, but he had every intention of trying.

"Chairmen," Ray said, smiling and nodding.

Cole knew that all of the thirteen Starburst ship's chairmen's images were on a split screen in front of Ray and Tacita.

"Data will follow this message about a discovery that has just been made," Ray said. "In short, it seems our branch of the Seeders is only one of six hundred different Seeder groups the ancients started over four million years ago."

Cole glanced at Echo who was just shaking her head. He couldn't even fathom that number. Over a billion galaxies had been seeded since Ray and Tacita started and each galaxy had billions and billions of human worlds.

That meant out there in the vastness of space there might be almost six hundred more Seeders groups working at the same pace.

Incredible.

And at a scale impossible to imagine as far as Cole was concerned.

Did the Seeders ever do anything on a normal scale?

Ray went on. "The information being sent to you is the locations, adjusted for galactic shift over the four million years, of the other seeded groups. Unlike with our group, which was the closest to the old home worlds, the ancients have not made contact with any other groups in four million years due to the vast distances involved. We were the only ones they stayed around and helped past the first Seeder ship."

"They don't know what's happened to the ancient seeded groups," Echo said softly.

Cole felt his stomach twist up. The history of the Seeders, this branch of Seeders at least, had been full of near-disasters. Not counting the major war they just had barely won. No telling what had happened to the other groups.

"So our new mission for the Starburst program is to find those other groups," Ray said. "We will decide on a group by group basis if contact will be wanted or required."

Ray took a deep breath and with a nod from her partner Tacita kept going. "The distances are so great to these other groups that even our five-hundred-year missions would have not reached the closest one."

Cole shook his head. He had tried to understand the distance they planned on traveling on the five-hundred-year Starburst mission. To say that all the other Seeder groups were far beyond that was impossible to grasp.

"So we need all Starburst ships," Ray said, "to pull in all scout and military ships and return on a direct course toward the Milky Way Galaxy at top speed. We will meet each ship within a year with a construction fleet to do upgrades on every Starburst ship."

"Upgrades?" Cole asked softly so only Echo could hear. He had no idea what kind of upgrades were possible.

Ray smiled, more than likely seeing the puzzled looks on every Starburst ship's chairman's faces.

"We will revamp the drives on every ship to a top speed of trans-tunnel forty-two and boost the shields to match. All information is being sent to you. Study it as you get turned around and headed back at full speed. We will be in direct contact with every ship over the next few days as to upgrade schedules."

With that the screen went back to scrolling data coming in from all the scout ships.

"*Data being received from Star Fall,*" *Star Trail* said.

Cole stared at the big screen for a moment, then glanced at Echo. Around them the command crew had broken into talking.

"How fast is forty-two?" Echo asked, glancing at Cole. "We can already go by an entire galaxy in an hour at a fourteen trans-tunnel speed."

Cole had no idea. Trans-tunnel drive opened a tunnel outside of space to allow ships to travel faster than light through the tunnel. Someone, a long time ago, had realized that if you opened more tunnels inside of already open tunnels, the speed increased by factors.

Before the war, it had taken a ship fifty years to get between galaxies. By the end of the war, the trans-tunnel drive at fourteen trans-tunnels opened inside of each other had allowed travel time between galaxies to be cut down to only hours.

For the last fifty years they had been traveling at transtunnel eight and had gone by millions and millions of galaxies.

Forty-two would mean they could get between galaxies in seconds for all he knew.

How far out were they going to go to find these other Seeder groups?

The idea of that kind of distance just scared him more than he wanted to admit.

CHAPTER 2

SEVEN YEARS LATER

Chairman Echo Guinn felt relieved, finally, that they were about to get started outward again. Exploring again. The last seven years had seemed to really drag more than any other stretch of years in all her life.

Instead of a constant thrill of exploring, going forward, they had reversed course for almost a year, then stopped for six years as all upgrades were done by fleets of repair ships as well as in factories onboard *Star Trail*.

Most of the crew had managed to get back numbers of times to their home galaxies over the repair time, but she and Cole had stayed onboard the entire time. This was their home, their life.

But they had taken some down time to explore the vast wild areas on the ship and to rest.

Now she stood beside Cole in the command center watching the big screen. *Star Trail* and all the thousands of smaller ships onboard had been modified and tested for the new top speed and with shields that could plow through the center of a planet and not even notice.

The thousands of military ships on board had been upgraded with new weapons systems and cloaking capabilities as well.

They were finally ready to go once again.

Outward into unknown space.

It had been decided a year ago that the Starburst ships, of which there were now twenty, since six new ones had been built and crewed over the last seven years, were to head directly toward the closest Seeder areas.

Star Trail was to be the first to start out, with the others heading in different directions over the next few months. They had over six hundred other Seeder groups to find. And the vast distances in the universe those six hundred were spread through wasn't possible to even imagine.

But to Echo, the speed they would be traveling also wasn't possible for her to imagine.

The plan now was to not explore the galaxies they passed along the way, but just head at near top speed for the closest Seeder location. Even with the new drive at trans-tunnel forty, the trip would take eight months to reach the closest Seeder area.

Galaxies would flash past like so many dots. Over the last seven years, they had developed ways to take sensory readings of all the galaxies as they went by, at least the closest ones. And if something seemed interesting, the plan was that a scout ship with a military escort would launch and go back to take a look.

Star Trail would remain at forty trans-tunnel speed, but the scout and military ships dropping back would chase *Star Trail* down after their survey was done by going at maximum speed of trans-tunnel forty-two.

It would take the scout ships a few months to catch up if they spent a full day surveying a galaxy, but they would.

She and Cole figured that in the billions of galaxies they would flash past, they would only deploy a few-dozen scout ships. That's how dead the universe was of intelligent life.

But what had everyone scared and excited was what they would find when they reached the Seeders area. *Star Trail* would be the first to do so of all the Starburst ships.

And that worried Echo more than she wanted to admit even to Cole.

"Ready?" Cole asked Echo.

He smiled that wonderful smile of his that she never grew tired of, but she could tell from his eyes that he was as worried as she felt.

She nodded and together they turned around to face their command crew.

"Scout ships with military escorts ready to launch?" Echo asked.

"They are," JP said.

JP was their second in command and the most efficient person Echo had ever met. He was shorter than her five-four height, but she had no doubt he was a lot stronger. He had a bald head that he kept shaved on purpose. He looked slightly round, but Echo doubted there was an ounce of fat on the man.

"We're going to flash past where we were seven years ago in about an hour," Cole said. "Sensing systems on line and ready? If so, here we go. Stand by."

He glanced at Echo.

She smiled at him and took his hand as they turned around and sat down in their command chair.

The chair molded in around them, giving them complete contact with *Star Trail*.

Heads-up displays appeared around them showing them the complete status of the ship. Echo loved sitting in the command chair with Cole. It felt like she was even closer to him than any other time. The two of them and *Star Trail* felt almost like one unit.

"*Star Trail*," Echo said. "If all systems are go, take us to trans-tunnel forty."

"*Jumping to trans-tunnel drive now,*" *Star Trail* said.

Both Echo and Cole watched every detail that came across the screen in front of them for the next hour until they went past the point they had turned around seven years before.

"*All scanning systems working and online,*" *Star Trail* said.

Echo could see that they were scanning a hundred galaxies to each side of their path. She didn't want to leave just yet as she watched the tally of thousands of galaxies flashing past, the number adding up more and more.

"*Scout ship and military ship launched,*" *Star Trail* reported.

Echo had seen that. The scout ships with military escort would launch automatically at the first sign of any life in a galaxy.

"Show us the data that caused that launch?" Cole said.

The image of a small spiral galaxy appeared on the screen. The data showed a clear sign of a medium-advanced civilization that had once tried to expand to a number of star systems but it seemed to be now extinct.

But it was worth a closer look, Echo had no doubt.

"At the old speed we wouldn't have run across that galaxy for another thirty years," Cole said.

Echo just watched the data as thousands and thousands more galaxies dropped behind them.

Not only was the space between galaxies vast, but most galaxies never gave birth to any intelligent life at all. And when it did, it rarely survived.

Humans, the Gray, and the Cirrata had somehow beaten the odds.

Echo wondered if they would find more races that had.

She wasn't sure if the idea scared her or excited her.

CHAPTER 3

EIGHT MONTHS LATER

C ole stood beside Echo near their command chair and watched the scans coming in from in front of *Star Trail*. They were now close to the location of the Seeders that the ancients had launched here. If the Seeders had come this direction with expansion, there might be galaxies in this area.

But so far no signs of any kind of life in any of the galaxies ahead.

Around them the command center worked at an almost silent intensity, only talking in hushed tones when needed.

Star Trail was at trans-tunnel twenty now, moving past galaxies one every minute. That was slow enough for the scans ahead to really work.

And *Star Trail* was also shielded completely. No one would be able to see it coming. Cole and Echo had decided to take no chances.

Almost all scout and military ships were on board at the moment as well.

Over the last eight months they had launched thirty-nine scout ships with military escorts to get closer readings on galaxies with possible life. All but five of those ships had caught up with them and were now back on board. The scout ships had found very little. Mostly just either growing cultures that had yet to leave their home planet or dead cultures that had managed to spread out a little before going extinct.

The other five scout ships would catch up within the next day at this speed.

Now everyone stood ready. No one knew for what, but they were all ready.

The other nineteen Starburst ships were also watching, as well as the ancients remaining in the old home area.

Cole and Echo had spent a lot of time poring over the old records from the ancients of this group of Seeders. The last contact this group had had with the ancients had been just under four million years ago, just as the Seeders had started to move out of their home galaxy and into others.

Six thousand, two hundred of the ancients had stayed behind knowing they would never see their home worlds again due to the slowness of the ships and the vast distance. No one believed that many of them would still be alive. But Ray and Tacita had lasted four million years, so it was possible.

Very possible.

From what Echo and Cole could see, there seemed to be nothing at all that made this group different from the early years of Ray and Tacita. But Ray and Tacita had the ancients helping them for centuries. This new group had no outside help at all other than the six thousand ancients embedded in the culture.

And four million years was a very long time.

Cole just hoped they would find a large, galaxy-spanning culture of humans that had been seeded.

But as each galaxy flashed past and there was no sign of any form of life at all, Cole got more and more worried. In twenty minutes they would approach the home galaxy of this branch of Seeders.

Cole felt the clock just ticking down as they got closer and closer. And around them the tension in the command center seemed to expand like a weight pushing down on the air.

No one in the control room around them said a word. Echo stood absolutely still, her hands behind her back, her intense gaze on the big screen in front of them.

Cole shifted his weight from foot to foot, like he was getting ready to take off running. He felt like he was swimming through the silence like it was deep water pushing him down.

Finally, with just a dozen galaxies left to go before the home galaxy, *Star Trail* said simply, *"Signs of terra-forming in the approaching galaxy."*

It seemed that everyone in the room exhaled at once.

"Stop near the edge of the galaxy," Cole ordered.

A few seconds later *Star Trail* said, *"Holding position."*

"Human civilizations?" Echo asked as she and Cole both stared at the data flowing over the big screen in front of them.

"No," *Star Trail* said.

Then Cole saw the data coming in that twisted his stomach.

"The Gray fill the arid areas of every terra-formed planet and the Cirrata cities fill the oceans," Cole said softly. "No signs of human inhabitation."

Echo nodded.

Cole could see that the scans were showing millions of Gray ships and Cirrata ships in flight throughout the galaxy. They all seemed to be moving at the old pre-war Seeder ship speeds that would take them weeks to get across a galaxy and years to get between even the closest galaxies.

"Dispatch fifty cloaked scout ships with military escorts," Echo said. "Surround this galaxy and get any information possible. Stay cloaked."

The ships had been standing by, ready to launch, and within a minute *Star Trail* reported all ships launched.

"Let's move on," Cole said, working to keep his voice calm.

Echo nodded.

He knew there were many explanations for what they had just found. In their area the Gray had home galaxies as well as living on all human worlds. And so did the Cirrata. And Gray and Cirrata had joined each group that the ancients had seeded. So seeing the Gray and the Cirrata was no surprise. They were supposed to be here. But so were the humans.

It bothered Cole that there was no sign of human inhabitation.

Bothered him more than he wanted to think about, actually.

On a direct path to the original seeded galaxy were eight other galaxies. They found the same at each. Bustling and seemingly healthy Gray and Cirrata civilizations filled each galaxy.

No humans.

Not even signs after four million years that they had been on any planet. Of course, after that long, there would be no signs left.

Cole and Echo left scout and military ships at each galaxy to do intense scans and gather information.

Then they flashed into a holding position near the original seeded galaxy.

The same.

No sign at all of humans.

Just Gray and Cirrata.

"Something went horribly wrong here," Echo said softly as the data came in.

Cole only nodded.

"*Star Trail*," Echo said, "Can you scan for any extremely ancient signs of human civilizations."

"*There are signs,*" *Star Trail* said. "*But nothing remains.*"

"Can you estimate, within a range, how far in the past the humans vanished?" Cole asked.

"*On only preliminary data,*" *Star Trail* said, "*approximately three-point-five million years ago. Possibly longer.*"

Cole glanced at Echo who was looking as shocked as he felt.

"*Star Trail,*" Cole said. "Recall all ships."

Echo nodded. Then she said softly, "This is out of our hands now."

"Exactly," Cole said. "The Gray from our area will need to make contact here if contact is even desired."

He had a hunch the Gray and the Cirrata that worked with them and the ancients wouldn't make contact. From what he could tell, this culture was stable. No point in bothering it now.

They would do a full scan of all the galaxies this culture occupied.

If the humans had actually vanished over three million years ago, there would be no evidence of what happened. This might be a mystery that might need to remain a mystery.

CHAPTER 4

cho and Cole had just finished lunch in their
apartment when *Star Trail* said simply, "Chairmen Ray
and Tacita request a conference."

Echo sipped on her coffee as Cole said, "Put them through
here."

Their apartment was large, with two offices and a large
bedroom and walk-in closets. The kitchen was wonderful, state
of the art, and their dining table was huge, usually half-covered
in books and work pads. Echo loved everything about it.

The living room was sunken and had soft couches and walls
full of books. A stone fireplace filled one wall of the living
room. They spent a lot of time there either reading or watching
movies.

The place had a college clutter level, as Cole liked to call it.
Mostly just books either just finished or to-be-read.

Their three cats, direct descendants of one of the cats they
had found on one of their missions on a destroyed planet,

napped in different areas of the living room. All three were shades of orange and white. None of the cats had even bothered to come into the dining room to join them for lunch. Typical cats.

There was a screen over their dining table and it flickered as *Star Trail* made connection with Ray and Tacita back in the Milky Way Galaxy.

As *Star Trail* had traveled the vast distance from the Milky Way, they had dropped off small stations, all pre-built and staffed with a crew of ten each. The stations were actually fairly large and comfortable with furnished apartments for hundreds and restaurants and a few bars on each station. The crew of each station rotated in and out every few weeks.

Seeders could teleport long distances, but not as far as *Star Trail* had traveled. Not even chairmen who could teleport the farthest could make that length of jump.

So they called the trail they had left of small stations breadcrumbs and any Seeder on board *Star Trail* could jump from station to station back to the Milky way if needed, stopping to sleep and eat at any station along the way. It normally would take three days to make the journey, but it was possible and many of *Star Trail's* crew were doing it at any given time.

Considering that there were over three million people on *Star Trail,* Echo was surprised that breadcrumb trail of stations wasn't more crowded than it was.

Star Trail had dropped over eighteen hundred breadcrumb stations. Those stations also allowed new crew to join *Star Trail* from the Milky Way and easy communications over the vast distance as well.

Every Starburst ship was creating a breadcrumb trail out

into the distances of space. Echo actually considered those trails to be one of the most important things they were doing. On board *Star Trail* they had six factories that covered many, many square kilometers, working at full speed to build the stations and get them ready to drop.

At any given point they had over a hundred stations just waiting with more being built and completed right down to the furniture. They were built on a pace of one station per five hours. Every Starburst ship had the same capability.

Here in this culture of Gray and Cirrata, they would drop off a much larger and very shielded station for those wanting to come and research and watch this culture as well as a smaller station near each occupied galaxy.

After a moment, as Cole cleared off the last of their dishes from the wonderful French Dip sandwiches they had had for lunch, Tacita and Ray appeared on the big screen behind their dining room table.

"Ancients have any idea what happened here?" Cole asked.

Echo was hoping that they did.

Both Ray and Tacita shook their heads. Echo could tell that both were very bothered by what had been found. As was everyone on board *Star Trail*. They had gone looking for long lost cousins and found them all dead or missing. That would clearly upset anyone.

It wasn't doing her any good at all, that's for sure.

"We have something you should know about that we have just been told by the ancients," Ray said. "The mother ships of the Seeders of four million years ago all had hidden tracking devices built into them."

Echo shook her head as Cole laughed.

"Four million years is a long time for a ship to survive," Cole said. "Let alone a tracking device to still work."

"Ask *Star Trail* if she could survive that long?" Tacita said.

Echo said, "*Star Trail*, could you survive in space for four million years in your old mother ship form? Before you became a Starburst ship?"

"*Yes,*" Star Trail said. "*It would not be difficult.*"

"Shit," Cole said, standing and facing the screen.

Echo moved over to stand beside him.

Ray and Tacita looked extremely serious.

"When the ancients pulled back from the area you are in, the Seeders there had three mother ships," Ray said. "Their names were *Sun Hawk, Sun Hunter,* and *Sun Heaven.*"

"Find them," Tacita said, "And we may find out what happened to the Seeders and humans in that area of space."

"We are sending the information to *Star Trail* that would be needed to track them through long distances," Ray said. "And through the years."

"Good luck on this," Tacita said.

And the screen went blank.

Cole laughed and went back to the sink to put the dishes in the dishwasher.

"What's so funny?" Echo asked. She clearly didn't find any of this funny.

Four hundred years earlier they had been stationed on a human planet mostly wiped out by a rare electromagnetic pulse. Their work for those years had never left either one of them and now here they were finding another culture destroyed. This was bringing back memories of those years for her and she knew it was for him as well.

"I was kind of hoping," Cole said, "that we could just move onward and leave this mystery for someone else to solve."

Echo agreed with that. She had been hoping the same thing.

Desperately hoping to get away from what seemed to be massive death of more billions of humans than she ever wanted to think about.

But that wasn't going to be the case, clearly. Somewhere in this vast area of space were three Seeder mother ships.

Very, very old ships.

Now the question was where.

SECTION TWO

THE SEARCH

CHAPTER 5

E cho had come up with the idea that the best way to start to find three four-million-year-old Seeder mother ships was to map the area they had seeded.

Cole liked the plan only because it would give them more data, not because he thought it would help them figure out where the ships were in this vast area of space.

Star Trail had scanned the immediate area around the home galaxy and found no trace of the three ships. So they had launched eight hundred scout ships with military escorts to go out from the center and discover which galaxies had been seeded.

Now Cole stood next to the command chair, sipping his morning coffee, watching as the results started to come in from the scout ships.

No sign of any human in any galaxy had been found in three days of exploring outward. That really bothered him more than he wanted to let on. Something horrid had happened and they were sitting here with a ship full of three million Seeders, basically human in all respects except for a few genetic details. Somehow they needed to figure out what had happened.

"Star Trail," he said, "please put on the large screen a three-dimensional map of the galaxies that were seeded. Make the seeded galaxies green, the ones not seeded or that we have not explored yet white."

On the big screen thousands of green dots appeared surrounded by many more white dots. A clear pattern was emerging from the exploration.

The three mother ships had gone in three different directions from the home galaxy.

Just as Ray and Tacita's ship had done from their home galaxy, the seeded galaxies formed a trail as the mother ships jumped from one seeded galaxy to the next closest galaxy.

Three trails led away from this home system, each with hundreds of galaxies. About as many as could be seeded in a half-million year's time. But now the scout ships were starting to find the end of the trails. That much was becoming clear as well.

Whatever had happened had spread from galaxy to galaxy. How was that even possible?

Cole knew of nothing that would even make that possible.

Cole sipped on his coffee and watched as ship after ship reported in, firming up the map on the big screen. All three original Seeder mother ships had made about the same progress and all three had clearly stopped at about the same time.

Star Trail was constantly scanning through every scout ship for any sign of the three mother ships.

Nothing.

Echo appeared beside him. She was freshly showered from her morning exercise and smelled faintly of apricot shampoo. She had on a white blouse with her sleeves rolled up and jeans.

She had two cups of coffee in her hands, handing him a fresh cup.

He smiled and said, "Thanks."

It was part of their normal morning routine, one that he loved. Just being beside Echo made him happy no matter what they were doing.

"I see the map is almost filled in," Echo said.

"Afraid so," Cole said. "*Star Trail*, approximately how many galaxies did the three Seeder mother ships seed?"

"*From the pattern,*" *Star Trail* said, "*the total will be just under eight thousand galaxies.*"

"Thank you," Cole said. Then he turned to Echo. "There had to be over a billion human planets in each one of those galaxies. How did that many humans vanish? We need to find the answer to that."

Echo nodded, staring at the big screen. "We need to find those three ships or at least what happened to them."

Cole suddenly had an idea. "*Star Trail*, would you contact Ray and Tacita and have them ask the ancients if the three mother ships might have known about the ancients' existence even though their crew did not."

"*Question sent,*" *Star Trail* said.

"What are you thinking?" Echo asked.

Cole just shrugged. "If those three ships didn't know about

the ancients, they would act one way. If they knew, they would act another way. That's all."

Echo smiled. "Very good thinking."

"On this puzzle we need all the help we can get," Cole said. And he believed that.

As they watched, the scout ships sent back in reports from beyond the last seeded galaxy. No sign of any seeding and no signals at all.

On the screen now were the results of over a half-million years of Seeder work, now only occupied by the Gray and the Cirrata. And there was no doubt that after over three million years, neither of those cultures would be able to help at all even if contacted.

The Gray and the Cirrata didn't live as long as Seeders. In fact, normal Gray and Cirrata had life spans not much longer than humans. No chance after three million years of any memory that would help would survive.

Cole doubted they even would remember another culture built their worlds for them.

Cole glanced at Echo. "I suppose we need to take the next step."

She nodded. Then said, *"Star Trail,* please show at scale a three-dimensional representation of how far the three mother ships could have traveled at their top speeds since the last galaxy was seeded here."

A sphere appeared on the large screen. Billions of tiny dots, each representing a galaxy filled the sphere.

Cole just shook his head. That was a vast, vast area of space and those three ships or the remains of them could be parked anywhere in it.

"*Star Trail*, are any of the other ancients-planted Seeder cultures close to this sphere?" Echo asked.

"*No*," *Star Trail* said simply.

Once again Cole was shocked at the vastness of space.

"How long at trans-tunnel forty would it take scout ships to reach the edge of that sphere from here?" Echo asked.

"*Three weeks*," *Star Trail* said.

Cole just stared at the vast sphere, shaking his head. It would have taken those mother ships three and a half million years to travel what *Star Trail* and all the scout ships could now do in three weeks.

They stood in silence as the command crew worked around them and more and more information came in from the scout ships.

Cole knew what they needed to do next. He and Echo and their top command crew had talked it over and then presented the idea to Ray and Tacita who had agreed.

"Seems it is time to start the mini-starburst project," Cole said.

The project simply put was to launch almost every scout ship they had, about eight thousand, all with military escorts, in a starburst pattern from *Star Trail*, all going at top speed outward to the edge of where the three ships might have gone, all searching for the signals from the three ships.

Ray and Tacita had assured them that the signals would still be functioning even if the ships had been destroyed.

Cole just hoped that was right.

Echo nodded. "*Star Trail*, call in all ships. We launch the mini-starburst project tomorrow."

Cole stared at the sphere on the screen in front of him. That was a vast amount of space to search. And his biggest worry was that they would find nothing.

He almost dreaded that more than he dreaded finding the ships.

Almost.

CHAPTER 6

The answer came back from the ancients on the question Cole had asked. The three lost ships might have known about the ancients. And for one large and glaring reason. There was a chance there had still been ancients alive at the point the humans vanished.

Cole just shook his head. He and Echo had completely forgotten that one not-so-small point. The ancients had stayed behind with this group and more than likely would be on the mother ships.

When they got the answer, he and Echo had been just finishing up dinner in their apartment. Cole had made them a spicy taco salad and they both had been sipping on some sort of special beer.

They liked to have a drink every evening to relax, usually right after dinner before going to their offices to work or moving to the living room to watch a movie. Neither of them drank more than one glass of wine or beer or one cocktail a day, but they enjoyed the ritual of it more than anything.

And they had made a game out of making the drink appropriate to the meal as much as possible. Tonight they were sipping on a beer that tasted so light and watery that Cole actually didn't much care for. But one of the command crew had told him it went well with tacos and taco salad.

He honestly wasn't so sure and from the way Echo sort of stared at the light golden color of the beer, she wasn't sure either.

"Saved from the beer by work," Cole said, pushing his still-full glass toward the center of the table.

"Thank heavens," Echo said, laughing and putting her glass beside his. "Tasted like colored water. Bad colored water."

"Tequila next time with tacos," Cole said. "Margaritas."

"Now that I would drink to," Echo said, smiling.

He loved it when she smiled. They were both under stress and the idea of having to find three mother ships that each had had over a million people on board bothered them. But they still managed to stay level, she more than he, of that he had no doubt. She was the rock in the relationship.

But she thought he was, so it seemed to work out fine.

Now the answer they had gotten back from the ancients changed how they needed to look at everything.

"*Star Trail,*" Cole said, "Could you please find out the top speed of the ancient ships when this area was seeded."

"*The ancient seeding ships that came here used trans-tunnel twenty,*" *Star Trail* said.

"You think the ancients might have helped them pick up speed?" Echo asked.

"If they were running from something," Cole said, "I sure would."

"*Star Trail,*" Echo said, "would you please ask through Ray and Tacita if any of ancients left here knew the locations of the other seeded groups closest to this one? And also get an exact list of the ancients left with this group if they have it. Their specialties if any. That sort of detail."

"*Contacting Chairmen Ray and Tacita,*" *Star Trail* said.

"What are you thinking?" Cole asked, smiling at his beautiful partner.

"Four million years or so ago the ancients started building a new home, didn't they?" Echo asked. "About the time this expansion started."

Cole nodded. That was at least what they had been told. All this was information that *Star Rain* and the other Starburst ships had found out when they made contact with the ancients left in the old home area of space, an area abandoned much like what they were finding here.

"And a million years ago the ancients supposedly all moved to that new home, wherever it might be," Echo said. "Right?"

Cole sort of felt a shock hit his system. "You think all these humans on these billions of planets simply packed up and left?"

Echo shrugged, but kept smiling. "The ancients' home area of space was millions of times larger than this area. It would be possible. Remember, Seeders never think small and ancients make us look like ants in their universe."

The ancients had built a massive structure they called "The Center" that was their home. It was five spinning rings and the entire thing was larger than the Milky Way Galaxy. Cole had seen and studied pictures of the place and still couldn't grasp its size.

Cole thought for a moment. Her idea made as much sense as anything they had come up with so far. And he liked the idea of the humans moving a lot more than something killing them all.

He reached for her hand. "Leave the dishes. Let's go back to the command center to do some calculations."

She nodded and a moment later they appeared near their command chair. Behind them the second command shift was working and no one seemed in the slightest bit surprised that they had arrived. They often came back to work at odd hours.

Cole looked up at the data flowing over the big screen. Almost all scout ships had returned. Everyone was preparing for the big launch tomorrow.

"Star Trail," Cole said, "would you please show a sphere on the big screen with the distance the three mother ships might have traveled at trans-tunnel twenty in three-point-five million years."

A large sphere appeared that seemed to be filled with a film of white. Cole knew that every tiny dot that made up that film in that sphere was a galaxy. He couldn't even imagine the distance he was looking at. Numbers never helped him grasp such massive distances.

"Show with bright green dots," Echo said, "the other close areas seeded by the ancients if any are inside that sphere."

Many, many green dots appeared in one area of the sphere. Too many for Cole to count quickly.

"Star Trail," Cole said, "please show the location of the

Milky Way Galaxy with a bright white dot in relationship to this sphere."

A bright white dot appeared on one edge of the sphere.

Cole just stared at all of this.

"Shit," Echo said softly.

Cole looked at her. She seldom swore. She was intently staring at the sphere.

"*Star Trail,*" Echo said, "please show the ancients' old home world area of space as a bright red dot, keeping everything as best you can to scale."

The sphere shank just slightly and a bright red dot appeared.

Cole was starting to understand where Echo was going.

"*Star Trail,*" Cole said, "keeping everything as best you can to scale, show the other locations of all the seeded ancient cultures."

Over six hundred green dots appeared forming a half moon. The sphere included numbers of them.

"Look where the Milky Way and all of our seeded galaxies are," Echo said.

Cole just stared at the screen.

The pattern was very, very clear.

The Milky Way was directly between the ancients' old home worlds and the half-moon of six hundred seeded cultures.

And now, for the first time, Cole understood why the ancients wouldn't tell anyone where their new home was.

They were afraid of something.

They were afraid of something in these cultures they had seeded.

Cole glanced at Echo. Her beautiful blue eyes were huge as she stared up at him.

"What the hell is going on here?" she whispered.

He just wished he had an answer for her.

CHAPTER 7

W hy would the ancients hide tracking devices on the mother ships?" Echo asked, staring at the big screen in front of them. They had gone over and over everything they knew during the last hour and all it did was confuse them even more.

"I don't know, but we have got to tell the other chairmen," Cole said.

"Not the ancients," Echo said.

"No, from now on out they are out of the loop until we understand more."

Echo nodded. She agreed, but she wasn't sure exactly what they needed to tell the other chairmen. Granted, the pattern of the seeded areas was alarming at best.

And what worried her more than anything else was that the one Seeders group the ancients spent a few million years helping was the one directly between the ancients' old home worlds and where the other groups had been seeded.

That group standing like a wall was the Milky Way Galaxy Seeders. Their group.

It sure made the fact suspicious that the ancients wouldn't tell them where their new home area of space was located. And it sure brought more possible reasons for the ancients moving from their old home besides outgrowing the old area.

But what was happening here?

What could the ancients possibly be afraid of over millions of years?

So many questions, no sign of any answers.

She and Cole had spent the next hour, after discovering the pattern, working with the command crew to get more data. But there just wasn't much they could do.

At that point *Star Trail* said, *"List of the known ancients left in this area has arrived. Also, the ancients here knew the locations of the other seeded groups."*

Everyone in the command center heard that and just stood silently.

Echo didn't know what to think. But she knew her stomach was twisting which usually meant they were into something over their heads.

Cole just stared at the big screen shaking his head.

"I think we have two choices," Echo said, finally turning to face him.

Cole nodded.

"We go ahead with the mini-starburst search mission tomorrow as planned."

"Second choice?"

"We head at top speed for the next seeded area."

Cole nodded. "I think we have a third choice."

She looked at him with a frown, but indicated he should go on.

"We wait for two days until *Star Ray* arrives at their destination. If there are no humans left there, we know something bigger is going on and we head on to the next seeded area. If they find a normal seeded culture with humans, we do the mini-starburst search pattern to look for the ships here."

She nodded. She liked that plan.

"Who knows," Cole said. "That seeded area is inside the distance the three mother ships might have traveled. Maybe *Star Ray* will find them there."

She looked at Cole and smiled. "You really don't believe that, do you?"

He laughed. "Not a chance in hell. Just trying to stay positive."

She shook her head and kissed him and then they went back to sifting through all the data that had come in.

It was going to be a long two days of waiting that was for sure.

CHAPTER 8

Yesterday, Cole and Echo had decided to tell the other chairmen on the other nineteen Starburst ships their theory in a vast conference call. The big screen in the command center had shown all the other couples and their expressions as Cole and Echo laid out the patterns.

Cole found it amazing how many of the other chairmen jumped right to the same point he and Echo had gotten to. Something far, far larger was going on.

No one had any idea what, but it seemed clear something had happened four million years ago to cause this pattern.

Everyone agreed to not mention this at all to Ray and Tacita yet, since it was all just strange supposition and worry. Besides, Ray and Tacita were directly connected to the ancients.

One chairman pointed out that it had been the ancients who helped them get the faster speeds to go find out what was happening with these other seeded areas.

"Free scouting missions," another chairman had said and everyone nodded to that.

The agreement was that nothing would be said until *Star Ray* reached the next seeded area within reach.

So now Cole stood beside Echo, watching the feed coming in from *Star Ray* as it approached the home galaxy of an ancient seeded group. Lisa and Jaden, the two chairmen had their image in the lower corner of the feed.

Cole liked them both. He and Echo had spent time with Lisa and Jaden as their two ships were being overhauled.

Lisa stood almost six feet tall and was thin as a post, with long black hair and piercing green eyes. She loved to pull pranks on people and her laugh was infectious.

Jaden was Lisa's height but didn't look it because of his wide shoulders and shaved head that gave him a tough look. He had hands that looked like they could crush anything, but it turned out he was gentle and one of the smartest people Cole had ever met.

Over the years of the refitting of their ships, the four of them had made it a habit to go out every week to a different restaurant, sometimes light-years distant from where they were living. The four of them had made it a game and great fun to never repeat a restaurant. And they found some wonderful food and some wonderful experiences, often tied into not-so-wonderful food.

Cole missed those dinners and the diversity of being able to find so many different forms of restaurants. It was partially why he and Echo changed their meals regularly and experimented with both food and drink. They had grown to like it.

And Echo often talked with Lisa and Jaden about a meal

they had made. If he and Echo had best friends in this new world, it would be Lisa and Jaden, even though at the moment, the two ships were impossible distances apart.

Just as happened with *Star Trail*, Lisa and Jaden found terraformed galaxies about eight galaxies away from the original galaxy. But no evidence of human life.

Over the next few hours as *Star Ray* approached the home galaxy, it became clear that it would repeat what *Star Trail* had found.

And when the home galaxy of that group of Seeders was scanned, it also showed only a stable society of Gray and Cirrata, but no sign of humans.

"That group also had three mother ships as well," Cole said, glancing at Echo who looked more worried than he had seen her look before.

"So we now have humans completely missing," Echo said, "from more billions of human planets than I want to try to imagine."

"What in the world happened?" Cole asked.

At that moment *Star Trail* said, *"Ray and Tacita are asking to speak to all ships."*

"Link us in," Echo said.

After a moment Ray and Tacita's faces appeared on the screen. They waited until all chairmen on all twenty Starburst ships were linked.

"The situation that *Star Ray* has found scared the ancients we are in contact with," Ray said.

"There is much they are clearly not telling us," Tacita said.

Cole was shocked at the anger clearly coming from Tacita. He always thought of her as cool and calm.

"Ask them what they are afraid of," Cole said.

"And why they won't tell us where their new home world is at," another chairman said.

"We did," Ray said, his voice cold.

"They said nothing," Tacita said.

"So we want every ship to be prepared," Ray said. "Full military alert as you move forward."

"We no longer believe the Seeder ships are lost or that anything happened to the humans in those galaxies," Tacita said. "We believe they all moved for a reason we do not yet understand."

"A reason having to do with why the ancients put them out there in the first place," Ray said. "We will continue the build up forces here and try to get answers from the ancients."

"Be on high alert," Tacita said.

Ray nodded and cut off the connection.

Cole felt shocked. Around them the command crew stood in silence.

"Feels like the world just shifted," Echo said.

Cole could only nod to that.

"*Star Trail,*" Echo said, "are all the scout and military ships on board?"

"*All ships are on board,*" Star Trail said.

Echo glanced up at Cole and he nodded. They needed to get moving now.

"*Star Trail,*" Echo said. "Top speed for the next seeded group location."

"And inform the other Starburst ships and Ray and Tacita of our movement."

"*Entering trans-tunnel drive,*" Star Trail said. "*The other ships have been notified. Star Ray will be jumping to full speed in two hours after leaving breadcrumb stations behind. It will also head to its next destination."*

"Thank you," Echo said. "Continue scanning for the mother ship signals."

"Just over four weeks to our next stop," Cole said. "It's going to be a long four weeks."

Echo said nothing to that. And he didn't blame her.

CHAPTER 9

E cho was surprised at how busy they had been in the last four weeks. Turns out the four weeks hadn't seemed to take that long after all. Almost every day one of the other Starburst ships approached their first target ancient seeded culture.

And every seeded home galaxy and culture was the same. All had spent a half million years seeding, then all humans and Seeders alike had just vanished, leaving thriving Gray and Cirrata cultures on the terra-formed planets.

And the three and a half million years since that point had effectively erased all traces of what might have happened or how it happened.

All the chairmen had conference called every day as new data came on board. It was actually Lisa and Jaden that came up with the idea that started to narrow down some things.

They had laid out all the known ancient seeded home galaxies in this area of space. They knew that at least twenty of them had been abandoned, since all twenty Starburst ships had found the same thing.

So Lisa and Jaden had tried to figure out among all the seeded areas what would be the center point if they were all migrating to one major spot.

Once the lines were drawn it became very clear where these cultures' new home worlds would be.

Since the ancients really liked to build large home areas, if all the populations had moved to that one area, it wouldn't be surprising.

The reasons, on the other hand, were unknown, and why the ancients wouldn't even talk any more about what was being found made no sense to anyone.

Star Trail was within one day of arriving at the second seeded area when Echo decided to ask *Star Trail* a question. It really wasn't a question she thought would have any meaning, but was just curious.

She and Cole were standing near their chair in the command center and the main shift was working around the room.

"*Star Trail*," Echo said, "Assuming ark ships the size of a Starburst ship, how many such ships would it take to evacuate one normal human planet?"

"*Assuming a population of six billion humans on a planet,*" *Star Trail* said, "*assuming three million per ship, it would take two thousand ships of this size to evacuate a planet.*"

Cole sort of shook his head at hearing that and then asked, "*Star Trail*, would the resources be available in each solar system to build that many Starburst-sized ships?"

"Yes," Star Trail said. *"If the military and scout ships were not also built at the same time."*

"So per galaxy we are looking at a billion planets times two thousand ships per planet," Echo said. She couldn't even grasp that number.

"Even with round trips," Cole said. "That's just not possible. Even at the scale the ancients worked at."

Echo nodded. "We are missing something major."

Cole nodded and the two of them stood there staring at the screen watching the scanning data come in. Neither one of them had a clue what they were missing.

Nothing about any of this made any sense.

And it hadn't from the beginning.

Echo could feel her tension climbing. In less than twenty hours they would be at the second seeded home world. So she offered to cook them a good dinner and let them try to get some sleep.

Or at least rest.

She had just taken out some freshly made rolls from the oven and put them in a basket to go with the fresh turkey and gravy and stuffing she had made when she finally realized what they had been missing.

Cole was sitting at the kitchen table sipping on a glass of red wine when she put the rolls down in front of him and pointed at them.

He smiled up at her. "They smell wonderful. You want me to eat one?"

She laughed. "I do, but first take one and break it open. Don't burn your fingers."

He took one out of the basket and over his plate he broke it open, then took a deep sniff of the wonderfully smelling fresh bread.

"Now put it back in the basket," she said.

"This some sort of kinky form of torture," he said, laughing but doing as she said.

She pointed to his plate. "What do you see there?"

He glanced down. "Breadcrumbs. I have..."

Then he stared at the crumbs for a moment, then smiled at her.

"You think they used a breadcrumb-like network to move all those people?"

She nodded, smiling.

"We eat first and then see if we can work out where the network would be exactly," Cole said, pushing his glass of wine away.

Echo had to admit, the dinner was good, but never before had they eaten so quickly and left such a mess in their kitchen when they jumped back to the command center.

CHAPTER 10

ole had *Star Trail* work on figuring out where a breadcrumb trail would be from the Seeded area they were approaching that would lead to where they were guessing everyone had gone.

A dotted line appeared from the group of galaxies ahead.

Cole just stared at it. If the group ahead turned out to be as expected and that all humans had vanished over three million years before, they would search for that breadcrumb trail. Signs of it might still be in existence.

Echo stared at the image, nodding, then she asked a question Cole hadn't even started to think about.

"*Star Trail*, how long would it take to breed the Seeder genes into dominance in everyone in a planet's population?"

At that question the entire command center around them dropped to silence as the idea of what she had just suggested struck home.

"*Approximately two-hundred-thousand years,*" *Star Trail* said, *"assuming a normal population of four billion per planet. But as the Seeders genes became dominant the population would stabilize, since children are unusual in Seeders. So assuming a population of one billion per planet at full Seeders gene dominance, less than one-hundred-thousand years."*

"Would that be possible to do?" Cole asked.

"Yes," Star Trail said.

Cole felt his stomach just clamp up around the wonderful dinner he had just had.

"They are here and watching us," Echo said softly.

"We have been played for the fools," Cole said, understanding exactly what she was saying.

They were pawns in a much larger and very ancient fight among ancients. And she and Cole had just come in thinking they would find backwards Seeders cultures.

"Star Trail," Cole said, "Get all Starburst chairmen and Ray and Tacita on a conference call."

"Working," Star Trail said.

It took almost a full minute before everyone was linked together. Some of the chairmen had clearly been in bed. All the Starburst ships had agreed to run on the same schedule, so even though this was evening, some early-to-bed types had already retired.

"Ray, Tacita," Cole said, "are you away from the ancients?"

"We are in the Milky Way on our mother ship," Ray said, nodding.

Cole nodded and went on to explain their theory of the breadcrumbs trail of evacuation and what they had discovered on the timeline to create entire planets of Seeders.

Some of the chairmen just looked angry at the idea.

Then Cole said to Ray and Tacita. "I believe we have been played by the ancients in some ancient fight. And I don't much feel like being the pawn anymore."

All of the chairmen on the screen nodded to that.

Ray and Tacita nodded.

Cole knew exactly what needed to be done and needed to be done instantly.

"Suggestions?" Ray asked.

"Chairmen, please go to your chairs and close down this discussion to only ourselves," Cole said. "No command crew please."

Everyone nodded and Cole and Echo moved to their chair and sat down, letting the chair close in around them.

"*Star Trail*, please remove this discussion from the large screen, contain it only here," Cole said.

"*Done*," *Star Trail* said.

All other chairmen were linked in including Ray and Tacita.

"I believe we have two things we need to do quickly," Cole said. "We need to first, without drawing attention to what we are doing, find a number of the breadcrumb trails and figure exactly where the new home worlds will be."

"Agreed," Ray said and all the other chairmen nodded.

"We need to monitor all communication back along our breadcrumb trails of all of our crew," Cole said.

There were audible gasps from some of the other chairman.

"You suspect that crew on each ship is spying for the ancients?" Ray asked.

"No," Cole said. "I believe there are ancients on these ships with us. They are Seeders, as we are."

"*Star Trail*," Echo said, "Is there any way to tell the difference between an ancient and a Seeder from our seeded group?"

"*Yes*," *Star Trail* said.

"Are there ancients on board this ship now?" Cole asked, surprised at *Star Trail's* answer.

"*Yes*," *Star Trail* said. "*Just over seven thousand.*"

Cole looked at the shocked faces of the chairmen on his screen. "I'm sorry for this but we have to know. *Star Trail*, would you please have each Starburst ship check to see if any chairman of a Starburst ship is an ancient."

Star Trail said after a moment. "*Every chairman taking part in this conference is a Seeder from the Milky Way Galaxy group. But every command crew on every ship has an ancient.*"

Cole was about as angry as he could be. And clearly, looking at the faces of the other chairmen, he wasn't the only one. Being a pawn in someone else's game was never fun.

"So what do you suggest needs to be done?" Ray asked. He also sounded angry and from the look on Tacita's face she was about to explode.

"We send them home," Echo said. "We would have welcomed them if they had been honest with us from the start, but we can't trust hidden spies. We clear each ship of them quickly."

Everyone agreed.

"And we set up monitoring systems," Tacita said, "along each breadcrumb trail to each of our ships so no ancient can come through."

"All of our ships will be set up to monitor any communication as well that might be suspicious," another chairman said.

"We will pull all of our people back from the old home world of the ancients as well," Ray said.

Cole nodded to all of that. But he had one more thought that he hated.

"The ancients put tracking devices on every Seeder mother ship in these seeded areas," Cole said. "All of our ships need to be completely checked as well for such a device."

Every chairman nodded.

"Good luck on the purge, everyone," Cole said.

And with that he cut the communication and he and Echo, still in their command chair, went to work on how to escort each ancient off the ship and back along the breadcrumb trail.

It was going to be a very long night.

CHAPTER 11

E cho was the most saddened to learn that their second in command, JP Horshaw was an ancient. But she was happy to see that he was the only one on the main command crew who was.

They decided to first get with the head of the military. All of his men and women were cleared. It seemed the ancients did not do well in the military.

They next invited JP to their apartment. They had three armed military personnel standing guard and *Star Trail* put a shield around their apartment after JP jumped to their dining room. The shield that wouldn't allow him to jump away or contact anyone.

So Echo and Cole both cleared off the remains of their dinner dishes and had JP sit at the dining room table.

They offered him a drink and he picked his normal coffee. Many, many times over the last decades of time the three of them had sat at this table and talked and planned. JP had been with them from the start.

"So we have a question," Cole asked, sitting across from JP

Echo sat at the table and the three military guards were out of sight in the bedroom and hall and living room area.

She couldn't look JP in the eye. She felt completely betrayed and very angry.

"Why didn't you tell us you were an ancient?" Cole asked.

JP jerked, then nodded and sat back.

"You know we would have welcomed you aboard in the same way," Echo said.

"I know that," JP said. "But we all have our missions."

Echo didn't want to hear that, not in the slightest.

"So now that you will be leaving us," Cole said, "you want to give us a hint about your mission?"

"To report back as to what you found," JP said, shrugging.

"We have already been doing that," Echo said. "Why the secrecy?"

"Because," JP said, "those in charge do not believe that a younger society such as yours can deal with having ancients around."

"Well," Cole said, "they are right about that, because you old folks can't be trusted, clearly."

JP nodded. "It sure appears that way, doesn't it?"

"So what in the world has your people so afraid of what we are going to find out here?" Echo asked.

"Exactly what you are finding," Cole said. "The ancients who were put out here to seed these cultures all believed that humans should be simply bred out of the equation."

"Ancients do not?" Echo asked.

"No," JP said. "We would approach the Seeders in different cultures and worlds that appeared naturally and give them the opportunity to have their Seeder genes become active or remain as humans. Many, in fact most, chose to stay human. And the Seeder genes remained a rare occurrence."

"So what do you expect we will find when we locate this central home of this batch of Seeders?" Cole asked.

"We honestly do not know," JP said. "That's why so many of us are on these ships."

"Couldn't trust the kids, huh?" Cole said.

"Pretty much," JP said, nodding. "Not even enough to tell you we were here."

"Well," Echo said, "seems you all can go back to hiding in your new home, wherever that might be."

Echo didn't even try to keep the contempt out of her voice.

"Yup," Cole said, standing. "Seems the kids now got to go it alone without adult supervision."

He moved over and nodded for the military escort to come in.

Echo stood, staring at someone she had trusted for decades. "Your people might just want to worry about which side the kids decide to take when this is all said and done."

JP's face went white and he nodded.

A moment later JP and the three military men were gone.

And five hours later every ancient on board *Star Trail* was gone, headed along the breadcrumb chain under guard back to the Milky Way and then back to their own worlds, she was sure.

After this, she doubted the ancients would be much

welcome anywhere outside their own space, now that ships and security measures were set to scan for them.

After the last ancient was gone, the real search began for anything any of them might have planted, any tracking device, any communications device. Anything.

Star Trail was a vast ship that held over three million people and hundreds of thousands of other ships. That detailed search took them ten long days.

And it found hundreds of issues. For days, the anger and resentment to the ancients who had been tossed off the ship was almost at lynch-mob levels.

Eventually it calmed down as everyone slowly came to realize their world, *Star Trail,* was safe now. And that the other Starburst ships were safe. And all the ships back in the human galaxies were quickly becoming safe as well.

But that boiling anger at the ancients wasn't going to go away any time soon.

If ever.

Seeders lived a very long time and had perfect memories and Echo would never forget. She doubted anyone else on this ship would either.

Every Starburst ship had the same issues and all ships compared notes back and forth when something was found to make sure the same thing was found on every ship.

For the ten days, every Starburst ship had just stopped and held positions.

Every inch on the outside of *Star Trail* was scanned and the workings of all the screens and all the trans-tunnel drives were evaluated to make sure nothing could be traced in any fashion.

One minor adjustment had to be made to the trans-tunnel

drives of every ship. The upgrade to clear out a traceable problem had been sent to them from the Milky Way scientists. That adjustment took out a clear signature of the drive and also allowed them to increase all speeds to trans-tunnel forty-four.

As the search and adjustments were going on, every Starburst ship set new protocols on anyone coming and going through the breadcrumb trail. And every inch of every ship inside each Starburst ship was constantly scanned and rescanned.

Echo hated the new security measures, even though most on board the ships would never notice them. But after ten days and all the traps, tracers, and other things they had found installed by the ancients, she was glad the new measures were in place.

It was very disconcerting when those you thought were your friends had suddenly become an enemy.

CHAPTER 12

Cole had managed to keep his anger in check for the ten days of sweeps, changes, and new security measures. And now, as he stood beside the command chair drinking his morning coffee and studying reports as they came in over the big screen, he felt as if things might return to normal again.

Echo had decided she desperately needed her morning exercise and her routine as well. So she wouldn't be here for another twenty minutes at least.

He took another sip of his black coffee and then said, *"Star Trail*, please put on the big screen a logical meeting point for every possible direct breadcrumb trail from every seeded galaxy region the Startburst ships have explored so far."

"Parameters of the request?" Star Trail asked.

Cole thought for a moment, then said, "A large area of space with a vast cluster of galaxies, to start with. That area would need to be away from the Milky Way Galaxy in general,

83

beyond all of these seeded areas we know about in relationship to the ancients' old home area, and approximately equal distant from most of the seeded areas the Starburst ships have explored so far. Show the seeded areas as green dots that we have explored and dashed lines as logical bread crumb paths to a new central home area of space."

Behind him the command crew went silent as they all watched. Cole had no doubt they all needed to get past what had just happened. Looking and thinking about the mission ahead was one way to do that.

It seemed that almost everyone on the ship had known or been friends with an ancient. And a number had been married to an ancient. Two spouses chose to go with their partner. Three broke off the marriage when the ancient partner left.

Everyone on all the ships had healing to do, some more than others.

The image on the screen showed a vast area of space. The galaxies looked like faint mist on the big screen with twenty green dots in a half-moon shape.

Dashed red lines left each green dot and met in an area far, far beyond the green dots.

"Scale, please," Cole said. "Show as a bright orange dot the Milky Way Galaxy."

The image shifted down in scale slightly and a bright orange dot appeared near the bottom of the screen. Seemingly very close to the green dots.

"Using the distance from the Milky Way Galaxy to the first seeded area we reached, how far away is that possible area?"

"Eleven-point-three times farther," Star Trail said.

Cole was stunned at that distance. "At trans-tunnel twenty,

the speed of the old ancient ships, how long would it have taken them to reach that location from the location of the first seeded area?"

"*Over six hundred thousand years,*" Star Trail said.

"At trans-tunnel forty-four," Cole said, "how long will it take us to reach that location?"

"*Slightly under a year,*" Star Trail said.

He then had *Star Trail* show all of the six hundred seeded areas and with the same parameters to locate an area and show it.

Same area worked for all six hundred.

"Are there secondary areas closer?" Cole asked. "If so, please show them."

"*There are no other secondary areas closer that contain the mass and cluster of galaxies that would be needed to support the large number of human planets seeded in the six hundred areas if this pattern holds.*"

Cole just nodded and stared at the big screen and then tried to even comprehend the distances involved.

"So now we need to find the breadcrumb stations, if any of them still exist," Cole said. "To see if this theory has any validity."

He stared at the image for a moment longer, then said, "Thank you, *Star Trail.* Please resume with the reports on the main screen."

Around him the sounds of the command center going back to work slowly filled the room. He just stood, leaning against the railing, sipping his black coffee and staring at the reports of repairs and scans being completed.

If the ancients who seeded these areas had actually moved

to that distant location, it was clear they were very afraid of the main ancients.

The seeded cultures had used distance as a shield.

Unimaginable distances.

Then it dawned on Cole one thing they had been missing. Just as they had now sat up scanning for any ancients getting near this area or any area they were near, these areas they had just explored might have been monitored, even though abandoned.

That's what he would have done if he was that afraid of something coming after him.

And clearly, these ancients who had seeded these areas were very afraid.

For the next five minutes, he worked over ways of finding those scans, then when Echo arrived and handed him a fresh cup of coffee, he thanked her and indicated they should sit in their command chair.

She looked at him with a puzzled look, then set her coffee down and joined him in the command chair.

It closed around them and brought up the screens. Again he felt closer to her in this chair than at any point, almost as if the connection through *Star Trail* connected their minds in some way.

"*Star Trail*," Cole said before Echo could ask him any question. "Please make sure this conversation is not monitored in any fashion."

"*Understood and complying,*" *Star Trail* said.

"*Star Trail*," Cole said, "since by genetic development we were able to tell the slight difference between ancients and our seeded group, would it be possible to tell if we had any of the newly seeded groups on board?"

"*There was a high percentage chance that many of the ancients we removed were of the new groups,*" Star Trail said.

That stunned Cole and he sat back slightly.

"Because we removed all crew with ancient traits and the newer seeded groups would have the ancient traits?" Echo asked.

"*All personnel were removed whose traits did not match the Milky Way Galaxy group of Seeder traits that started in Chairmen Ray and Tacita's home world and on their Seeder ships,*" Star Trail said. "*The origin of such differences was not taken into account.*"

Echo nodded. "So they might have been other branches of ancients or they might have been from this area. Correct?"

"*Yes,*" Star Trail said. "*There would have been no way to distinguish the differences.*"

Cole felt a relief. That problem didn't need to be faced again with the safeguards they now had in place.

But his biggest worry still faced them.

"*Star Trail,*" Cole said, "using the information that the ancients gave us to track the hidden sensors on the old ancient mother ships, would it be possible to detect if we are being scanned without knowledge?"

"*Yes,*" Star Trail said.

"How long would it take to make the adjustments to equipment to discover any such scanning or tracking?" Echo asked.

"*Thirty minutes,*" Star Trail said.

"Please make the adjustments and search for any scans," Cole said.

"Also use any of the technology found planted on this and

other ships by the ancients and adapt it to find scans," Echo said.

"*Understood,*" *Star Trail* said.

Then, for the next thirty minutes, Cole showed Echo what he had come up with as a possible location for where all the humans on all the planets had gone.

"At that distance they could not use ships," Echo said, nodding. "And if they were all bread to be Seeders, the breadcrumb trail would be the only logical way."

"Only one problem," Cole said. "If I was afraid of the ancients as much as these groups seem to be, I would not only go a long distance away, but I would destroy any evidence of any breadcrumb trail leading in any direction."

Echo could only nod to that. "So the ancients that we have met moved their massive home area farther away in fear of something from this group."

Cole nodded.

"And this group possibly built a massive home area an incredible distance away in the opposite direction."

"Sure starting to seem that way," Cole said. "What in the world were they afraid of about each other?"

"You know," Echo said, "I used to think space was vast and impossible to explore. But now I feel like everything has tightened down and we are stuck between two ancient fighting groups and we don't even know why they are fighting."

"Both groups seem to be doing a lot more running than fighting," Cole said.

"And for that I am grateful," Echo said, smiling.

Cole very much was as well.

SECTION THREE

THE DISCOVERY

CHAPTER 13

Echo was relieved that they were not being scanned by any of the groups. At least as far as *Star Trail* could tell and the other nineteen Starburst ships had also worked to develop scanning to see if any of them were being scanned.

They were not.

So the next step was to start to search for any sign of a breadcrumb trail from any of the seeded areas. But Echo didn't give a lot of hope in that search. Even in open space, three and a half million years was a very long time.

But Cole felt that with all twenty of the Starburst ships searching, they would find some sort of evidence, if it was there, that the Seeders had used breadcrumb trails to move all of the humans on these planets.

"Nothing," Cole said one week after the search had started.

Echo could feel the frustration in his voice as she arrived

from her morning workout routine and handed him a cup of coffee.

Around them the command center hummed with its normal morning ritual and the reports flowing over the big screen now were search reports from thousands of scout and military ships dispatched from the twenty Starburst ships.

While she had been running, she had had a thought about the search and had expected this kind of result. They had been making some assumptions that clearly were wrong.

"Let's assume," she said, "that as the evidence points out, the Seeders from this area wanted to leave no trace as to where they were headed for the first group of ancients to find them."

Cole nodded.

"So we are assuming that they would have planted permanent breadcrumb stations as we did," Echo said.

Cole nodded again, then looked at her.

"My gut sense is that they used ships as jump stations with no intention of ever returning back to this area of space," Echo said.

"When the last person jumped past, they simply took the ship to the new home," Cole said. "I think you might have something there. It would explain why we are finding nothing. I was about to go back to the theory that they had all died off."

Echo felt her stomach twist at the thought she had when he suggested they all died off. She immediately went back to the memories of that planet she and Cole were stationed on with all the dead.

That had been their hardest assignment before being tapped to be chairmen of a mother ship and then a Starburst ship.

So just maybe this branch had died off. They seemed to be in a war with the ancients. Anything was possible.

She glanced at Cole. He was staring at the reports on the big screen in front of him, nodding.

"I need to talk with you," she said, pulling him toward their command chair.

He glanced at her, then nodded and they sat down, letting the chair close in around them.

"Something wrong?" he asked.

"I hope not," she said.

She wasn't sure exactly how to frame her question, so she started with a basic question. "*Star Trail*, it is my understanding that Seeders can live for a very long time. Correct? Millions of years if circumstances allow."

"*Yes.*"

"And that comes from a sequence of dormant genes in Seeders that can be activated. Without being activated, the Seeder would simply live a normal human lifespan. Correct?"

"*Yes,*" *Star Trail* said.

"Would it be possible to scan the data from each ancient that we found on board and that the other Starburst ships found on board their ships and determine if anything about that long-life sequence was altered in any of them to reduce the lifespan? And altered in a way that would not be easily noticed or discovered. Possibly by a form of damage."

"*Yes, it would be possible,*" *Star Trail* said.

"Please do so," Echo said. "While you are calculating that, please give me the standard birthrate for Seeders with activated genes."

"One child for every two-hundred-thousand Seeders," Star Trail said.

Echo knew that Seeders seldom had children. She didn't realize it was that seldom. There were a few births on the ship every month, but not many. Six of the children born on *Star Trail* had been born human with no Seeder's genes, so they and their parents had gone back to the Milky Way to give the child a regular life on a planet.

"Are you thinking that the ancients somehow altered the genes of the other ancients who came to this area?" Cole said.

"It would kill them off just as easily as fighting them," Echo said. "Given enough millions of years. Remember, JP said the ancients were worried about entire planets being bred to be Seeders only."

She hated the idea. That was why she had to clear it out of her head. And she had to make sure that everyone on board this ship was safe as well. At this point she put nothing past the ancients.

They wouldn't think of it as killing, only shortening already long life spans.

Damn she hoped she was wrong.

CHAPTER 14

Cole sat with Echo in their command chair, the command center around them completely blocked out, talking over possibilities as *Star Trail* scanned all the data collected from all the ancients they had kicked off the twenty Starburst ships.

He really hoped Echo was wrong, because as they waited, they ran over certain possible outcomes. And nothing either of them could think of sounded good.

Finally *Star Trail* said simply, *"I have the results of the question you asked."*

"Please summarize those results for us," Cole said.

"Two percent of the ancients removed from the Starburst ships had their Seeder genes damaged slightly, all in a similar and distinct fashion."

"Are the genes of any Seeder on this ship damaged in a similar fashion?" Echo asked a half second before he could.

"No," Star Trail said.

Cole let out the breath he didn't realize he was holding.

Beside him Echo nodded and looked relieved as well.

"So we had spies from these seeded groups on our ships as well," Cole said.

He wasn't sure how that was possible, but it sure seemed to be a logical assumption.

Echo nodded. "More than likely living with our group of Seeders since these groups started their big move over three-and-a-half million years ago. If we are right about where they moved to, the distance would be too great at the speeds they had to make it worth sending back spies."

"*Star Trail*, would you please trace all movements of the ancients with the damaged genes during construction and while here," Echo said. "I would like to know if they met with each other or tried to contact anyone outside this ship."

"*Understood*," *Star Trail* said.

"*Star Trail*, do you have a theory of how the genes were damaged?" Cole asked.

"*A long exposure to a low level of a certain type of radiation emitted by older trans-tunnel drives. The problem would have been easily remedied.*"

"Would the damaged genes be hereditary, passed down to Seeder children?" Cole asked.

"*Yes*," *Star Trail* said.

"What is the affect of the damage on a Seeder?" Echo asked.

"*None*," *Star Trail* said.

Cole just felt shocked.

"None at all?" Echo asked, clearly as shocked as he was feeling.

"*The specific damage I have found in the genes would have no affect at all on the Seeder,*" Star Trail said.

"So why did the ancients do this?" Echo asked, more to herself than Cole or *Star Trail*. "Assuming they did such a thing on purpose."

"*I have no theory as to the motivation,*" Star Trail said.

"They did it on purpose," Cole said, nodding. "I am sure of that." The reason was dawning on him and he hated it.

Echo looked at him. "Why?"

"They branded them," Cole said. "Just as we could kick the ancients off this ship by seeing the difference in our genes, they needed a way to track anyone from these groups."

All Echo could do was nod.

The ancients purposely damaged millions of people simply so they could be tracked.

Cole was really starting to hate the ancients.

CHAPTER 15

E cho and Cole sat over the dinner she had cooked. Chicken breasts in a light garlic sauce with steamed potatoes and some corn. She had to admit, this meal had turned out better than she had hoped. The sauce was a lot lighter.

The evening felt normal, which Echo loved. Even their cats were asleep in their normal places in the living room area.

It now had been a month since all the ancients had been kicked from all the Starburst ships and safeguards set up through the breadcrumb trail back to the Milky Way to let none of them through again.

Everything on all twenty Starburst ships seemed to have returned to a normal pace and the loss of friends and the hurt of being betrayed was fading. Seeders never forgot anything, so the memory wouldn't leave any of them. But they could get past it.

And it seemed most were.

Echo could feel herself putting the hurt and loss of JP away.

As of today, fifty-two of the seeded areas had been explored by the twenty ships. All of the ancient seeded areas were exactly the same. The human populations had vanished a long, long time before. At almost the exact same time in history.

"We're wasting our time now looking at all these seeded areas," Cole said, finishing off the last of his chicken. Then he pointed to his empty plate. "That was wonderful."

He took a sip of the oaked chardonnay she had picked out to go with the sauce and dinner and nodded, holding up the glass. "And this is perfect as well."

"Thank you," she said, smiling. "Going to have to remember how I did that sauce."

"Please," he said.

"So what do you suggest we do next?" Echo asked, finishing off the last of her chicken as well and letting it sort of melt in her mouth.

"I think we pull in all scout ships," Cole said, "and all twenty of us head for the first logical location where we think all these people would have gone."

She nodded and sipped her wine. She liked the idea, but it worried her on a number of levels, not the least of which was what they would find when they got there. Assuming they figured out correctly where millions of galaxies of humans had vanished to.

"Not agreeing?" Cole asked.

"Not disagreeing," Echo said. "Just worried. Feels like there is something we are missing."

She had no idea what that might be, but everything about this entire mission felt off.

"I agree," Cole said, taking a sip of his wine and then standing and starting to clean up the dishes. She just sat and sipped on her wine.

"What is haunting me is that Ray and Tacita said that the ancients were scared when we discovered no humans here," Echo said. "It was what they had been afraid of."

"That bothered me as well," Cole said as he moved the dishes toward the dishwasher near the sink. "But why I have no idea."

Cole worked in silence as she sipped on the wine.

Finally she asked, "Think we should check in with the other chairmen tomorrow to see if they think we should all spend a year going even deeper in space?"

"I do," he said. "But if we are going to do it, I think we should all meet up in this area of space and go as a fleet."

She nodded. "One more ancient seeded area will be reached tomorrow. If no change, we contact everyone."

"If one of them doesn't contact us first," Cole said, smiling. "Got a hunch we're all having this same conversation."

"I have a hunch that you are right," she said, laughing.

And he was.

The next morning, while she was still running along the edge of one of the ship's many forests in her morning exercise routine, *Star Ray* reached yet another abandoned seeded area of galaxies. Thirty minutes later Chairmen Lisa and Jaden called for a conference call and included Ray and Tacita.

Echo was called to the command center and when she appeared there, Cole was laughing.

"Great minds think alike," he said to her, then turned to the big screen. "*Star Trail*, please add us into the conference link with the other chairmen."

It took only another fifteen seconds before all the Starburst chairmen and Ray and Tacita were on the big screen. Twenty boxes. In each image Echo could see the command center crews behind the chairmen.

"I would imagine we have all been talking about this," Jaden said. Since he and Lisa had called the gathering, it was his place to lead it. His smile was wide and his shaved head almost gleamed in the light around him. "What should we do next is the big question?"

Ray nodded. "There is little doubt now that all seeded areas will be found abandoned by their human populations."

"Are we all pretty much in agreement with where we think they all went?" Jaden asked.

Echo nodded and beside her Cole did as well. All the chairmen on the screen nodded as well, without exception. She liked that they were all in agreement on this.

"On a direct path to the assumed target location," Lisa said, "It would take one year. But Jaden and I have another suggestion."

Jaden nodded. "*Star Ray*, please show the image of the suggested exploration paths of each Starburst ship. Show each location now with a green dot, show the target location with a red dot. Show the paths with a dotted line."

An image filled the screen replacing all of the faces of the other chairmen. It was a three-dimensional image of what looked like a sphere, but not a perfect sphere, more like a pumpkin shaped ball, with all the lines coming back in together at the red dot.

Echo could see the line from *Star Trail* leading off into unknown space and then circling around and back to the red dot of the target.

"We're out here to explore," Lisa's voice came over the image. "That's what these ships were built for. We think we should go exploring for some years on the way to our target. See what's out there."

Echo loved that idea. It sent a thrill of excitement down her spine just thinking of it.

Beside her Cole was nodding as well.

"That plan is being sent to all of the ships now," Jaden said as all the images of the chairmen appeared back on the screen.

"How long would it take to get to the target with these paths?" Ray asked.

"At trans-tunnel forty," Jaden said, "and dropping scout ships where we find interesting galaxies, it would take five years. At trans-tunnel thirty-six, which would allow scout ships more time along the way, it would take just over ten years."

Ray and Tacita both nodded.

"This plan would explore a vast area," Lisa said. "An area we really haven't even looked at in the slightest."

Almost all the chairmen on the screen were nodding.

"I suggest everyone study the plan and the details we have sent," Jaden said. "We meet again at the same time tomorrow morning."

Everyone nodded.

"Good," Jaden said, smiling. "See everyone tomorrow."

And the screen went back to scrolling reports.

Around them the command center started buzzing with excited conversations.

Echo turned to Cole, who was smiling.

"What do you think?" she asked.

"I love the ten-year plan," he said, smiling. "And I find it exciting again. Just exploring into the unknown."

"Getting reports from twenty ships exploring into the unknown," Echo said. "I find this idea wonderfully exciting."

"*Star Trail*," Cole said, giving her a hug and then turning to the big screen. "Please put up the image sent from *Star Ray* on one side of the screen and the data on the other."

Echo turned to the command crew behind them. "I want all of you studying this as well and any problems or opinions you might have before shift change today."

Everyone nodded. They all looked as excited as she felt.

Suddenly what had been missing was now back. This was a ship for exploration and exploring they were going again.

Finally.

CHAPTER 16

C ole was just about to head out on his afternoon run. He and Echo and the rest of the command center crew had gone over all the details about taking all twenty Starburst ships out to explore. Everything seemed fine and sounded exciting. There was no telling what might be out there in those millions of galaxies they would pass.

But something still felt wrong.

He leaned against their command chair, just staring at the large screen and information came over it giving him no help at all. Echo paced, just thinking, clearly not completely convinced at all either. She did that when she was bothered.

So he decided to do what a college professor had suggested he do when in doubt: Question all basic assumptions.

The first basic assumption was that one group of ancients was afraid of a second group of ancients. He could see no reason for that assumption. Nothing.

Sure, they had sent spies on this mission, but that didn't seem to be out of fear but more out of trying to find out what had happened out here.

The groups they were searching for had left ancient space over four million years ago. What kind of grudge would last that long? But Seeders did have the ability to remember just about anything.

So he decided to ask a question he should have asked back when the ancients were on the ship.

"*Star Trail,* what was the average age of the ancients who were on this ship?"

"*Two hundred and six thousand years.*"

Echo snapped around and looked at him, frozen in mid-pace.

"Repeat that please," Cole said, not really sure if he had heard the answer correctly or not.

"*Two hundred and six thousand years,*" Star Trail said. "*That is approximate to the nearest year.*"

"What was the age of the oldest and what was the age of the youngest?" Cole asked.

"*Seven thousand and four years was the oldest,*" Star Trail said, "*the youngest was ninety years of age.*"

Cole just felt shocked. In all his years as a Seeder he had never thought to ask some really basic questions about living.

"What is the overall average age a Seeder will live to?" Echo asked.

"*One thousand, three hundred, and eight years old,*" Star Trail said. "*Again that is an approximation of the average rounded to the nearest year of the data I have.*"

Silence filled the command center.

Complete and heavy silence.

Cole always felt that if lucky, he could live for millions of years. Now he understood suddenly it was going to take luck.

A lot of luck.

"What is the average age of the Seeders on this ship?" Echo asked.

"Four hundred and sixty years."

"Main cause of death of Seeders?" Cole asked as he tried to get his mind working again.

"Accidents," Star Trail said.

Cole nodded to that. They had had many, many deaths on *Star Trail* from accidents since they launched. It always seemed tragic, but it happened so often he hadn't thought much about it. After all, they had three million people on board.

"Second main cause?" Echo asked.

"Suicide," Star Trail said.

Cole again nodded. They had had numbers of those as well, but usually when someone started developing suicidal traits, they were sent back to the Milky Way for help.

Echo was looking almost haunted.

The silence around them felt unnatural. Clearly none of their command crew had thought to ask these basic questions either.

But now Cole needed another piece of information.

"Star Trail, with the information you have, how many Seeders, by percentage, will live to one million years of age? And beyond?"

"One-point-three percent," Star Trail said.

Now Cole knew what happened to the ancients they were looking for out here. But he had to hammer the nail in the coffin home just to make sure in his own mind.

"*Star Trail*, how many humans with Seeder genes would be born on a normal planet of four billion population in ten years?"

"*Approximately one thousand every ten-point-six years with a four billion population base.*"

"You multiply that by billions of human planets in any seeded galaxy and you have a lot of Seeders," Echo said. "Most don't have their Seeder genes activated."

Cole nodded. "Especially counting the fact that just in our group we have seeded a couple hundred thousand galaxies."

"Exactly," Echo said.

"*Star Trail*, how often do Seeders have children after their Seeder genes are activated?" Cole asked.

He knew the answer, but he needed to hear it one more time.

"*One child per every two thousand Seeders,*" Star Trail said.

Cole nodded.

Echo looked pale. A number of the command crew gasped lightly.

If these groups of Seeders had been stupid enough to breed only Seeder genes in the entire populations of these planets and activate them all, then they really did just die out.

They would not have had the human population bases to continue seeding, either, since seeding requires taking base material from a seeded planet and moving it to the next planet.

Very, very few Seeders would have lived long enough to be alive now.

But the real question was could they have been that stupid?

He didn't believe they could have been. Something else had happened.

And where did all those mother ships go?

CHAPTER 17

E cho now understood why the massive numbers of galaxies that had been the ancients' home world were empty. It wasn't because they had all moved out to a big new home. The ancients had told them that those galaxies had been only populated by Seeders and the home center had only had Seeders in it as well. Hundreds and hundreds of billions of Seeders.

And that the ancients had stopped exploring and seeding new galaxies with humans millions of years earlier.

The ancients had died off as well.

They didn't have a big new home. They had an empty old one the ancients were trying to keep maintained so that humans could once again live in it.

How could the ancients have been that stupid? What could have happened?

But now she knew that what they were facing wasn't two warring factions of ancients. They just had one faction, the original ancients hoping against hope that the other groups had survived. No wonder the ancients had feared exactly what the Starburst ships had found.

"We need to talk with Ray and Tacita," Echo said. "Get them to confront the ancients with this."

"And we need to tell all the chairmen this theory," Cole said.

Echo nodded. She knew Cole was calling it a theory, but it was the only theory that explained what they had found. In both the ancients' home area of space and in these seeded areas.

"Star Trail," Cole said. "Please ask all other Starburst ship chairmen to join us in a conference call. And invite chairmen Ray and Tacita as well."

"Invitation sent," Star Trail said. "Links are coming live."

"On the main screen," Echo said.

Within three minutes the other forty chairmen were present on the screen. Their command center crews were all watching behind them.

Cole glanced at Echo and she nodded that he should start.

"Matt and Carey," Cole said, "when you discovered the ancients' home area of space, it was clear that they had all left the planets about the same time in history. Correct?"

Matt and Carey both nodded.

"And when the eight of you talked with the ancients," Cole said, to the eight chairmen who had originally met the ancients, "they alluded to learning while trying to build a new home? Correct?"

All eight nodded.

"They would not, in any fashion, tell us where the new

home was," Ray said. "Even though we had been friends with a few of them for a very long time."

"Because they were embarrassed," Echo said.

"Why would they be embarrassed?" Tacita asked.

"Because they had to move back in with the kids," Cole said. "Their new home was with us."

"And we just kicked them out of it," Echo said. "For the moment at least."

The puzzled expressions on the forty faces on the screen almost made Cole smile.

"None of us did the math," Echo said.

Now the puzzled expressions just deepened.

"When you were talking with the ancients," Cole said, "didn't they say that all their home worlds had been only full of Seeders?"

"They did," Ray said, nodding.

"So let's do some math," Echo said. "*Star Trail*, what is the average lifespan of all known Seeders?"

"*One thousand, three hundred, and eight years old,*" Star Trail said. "*Again that is an approximation of the average rounded to the nearest year of the data.*"

Cole nodded. Those were the exact words *Star Trail* had said when they first asked the question.

"*Star Trail*," Echo said, "how often do Seeders have children after their Seeder genes are activated?"

"*One child per every two thousand Seeders,*" Star Trail said.

"In other words," Echo said, "doing the math, a planet of one billion Seeders would have a population of only five hundred thousand in one thousand years. And a thousand years after that only two hundred and fifty."

Stunned shock covered the faces of the chairmen.

A couple chairmen were nodding.

"It would be delayed by the small percentage of Seeders who lived past the thousand years," Echo said, "but not much."

"Those original home worlds of the ancients were not left for some bright shining home," Cole said. "The ancients mostly died off. Plain and simple. They stopped seeding human populations and they simply died off."

Ray was now nodding as well.

"They would have had no programs to seed humans without seeding human planets to start with," Tacita said. "If they stopped seeding human planets, that would have been lost."

Everyone was nodding. They all knew that the seeding programs were generated from galaxy to galaxy from previous human and animal stock. Once the ancients stopped seeding and only brought in Seeders, they were doomed.

Echo knew it was too stupid to imagine, but the evidence sure pointed to that reality.

"Chairmen Ray and Tacita," Cole said. "I think you need to confront your ancient friends, get the truth out of them, and if they tell you the truth, we need to invite the old folks back into our society."

Nods from most of the chairmen on the screen.

"We still have the problem of the vanished mother ships in all these seeded areas," Echo said. "Where did they go? And why? If the ancients are out in the open, telling the truth, they might be able to join us again and help us figure that out."

Ray and Tacita nodded.

"We will return with the truth quickly," Ray said.

With that they clicked off.

"Everyone check our math on this," Cole said. "We'll be back as soon as Ray and Tacita get us some real answers."

With that the screen went back to showing scrolling data about the status of the ship overall.

Echo turned to Cole. "Well, so much for a big exploration mission firing up."

"Yeah, back on the search again for missing ships," he said.

"And I really don't want to know what we will find in them," Echo said.

And she didn't. But what she really wanted to know was why and how the ancients would not understand the repercussions of activating all Seeder genes in a population.

There was no chance they were all that stupid.

Something else had happened and that unknown something scared her more than the idea of finding giant ships full of dead bodies.

CHAPTER 18

Cole was stunned that he had barely started into his morning coffee when Chairmen Ray and Tacita called a conference call.

"Star Trail, please have Chairman Guinn report to the command center."

Echo appeared at his side a moment later, a towel around her neck. She was sweating, but not much, so she must have just started into her routine.

"That was fast," she said, wiping off her face.

"Guessing they didn't get anything," Cole said. *"Star Trail,* please add us to the conference link and display it all on the large screen."

The other chairmen appeared on the screen as behind Cole and Echo the command center fell to silence. What they were about to discover might change what they would all be doing over the next decade or two.

"We are sad to report," Ray said after everyone was

connected, "that your theory as to what happened to the ancients is correct. They were keeping their big center functioning in hopes we would fill it once again, this time with humans."

Cole felt like he had been punched in the gut. It was one thing to have that idea as a theory, but to have it actually happen was another matter.

"Didn't they understand what would happen?" Echo asked.

"They did," Tacita said. "They had programs to up the birthrate among Seeders that eventually failed and at first they were still seeding human galaxies and bringing in Seeders."

Ray nodded. "There was that. But they did not count on one major change. Seeders starting living shorter lifespans."

Tacita nodded. "When we were born, over four million years ago, the lifespan of a normal Seeder was over a million years."

"There were fewer of us in any human population as well," Ray said. "But as galaxy after galaxy of billions of planets were seeded, the lifespan of a Seeder started to reduce. Slowly at first, but as the years went past Tacita and I and many others studied the problem. We found nothing wrong or any solution."

"And neither did the ancients," Tacita said. "But it spelled their doom. That's why they were so interested and sent so many along on these missions, in hopes of finding growing human and Seeder cultures besides ours."

"How many ancients are left?" Cole asked.

"Fifty million," Ray said, "most living in our culture and on one planet just outside the old home worlds. They rotate in and out of the command moon for the large center, keeping it maintained and waiting."

Cole just was stunned. A proud group now living in the bones of their greatest construction, doing everything in their power to keep it going in hopes someone would inherit the old home.

"So I suggest we lift restrictions on the ancients," Echo said.

"Everyone agreed?" Ray asked.

Cole watched as all chairmen nodded. No dissent or hesitations.

It seemed that now the forty chairmen of the twenty most powerful ships in all known space were the ruling body of humanity. At least for decisions like what to do with the old human culture now camping with them.

"So did you ask them about the missing mother Seeder ships?" Echo asked.

"We did," Ray said. "They have no idea and are worried."

Cole suddenly had an idea. "When these groups out here realized their mistake on activating all Seeder genes, would they have eventually returned to get more human stock to start the seeding process over?"

"Yes," Ray said. "The ancients have done that exact thing on the other side of their home area of planets. The have seven Seeder ships now going."

"Where did they get the human stock?" Echo asked.

"From our seeded planets," Ray said, shaking his head. "That was another thing they were very embarrassed about. They had to sneak in and take from planets enough animal and human stock to restart seeding."

"So there is a chance the old ships from these groups are still out there seeding?" Echo asked.

"Yes," Ray said, nodding. "There is a chance."

Cole just stared at all the faces. He had a hunch most of them were thinking the same thought he was.

How did they find them now?

SECTION FOUR

BACK ON THE SEARCH

CHAPTER 19

Echo stood beside Cole next to their command chair and studied the information coming in. All attention had now been focused back on finding the lost mother ships.

Echo and most of the chairmen were convinced that the old Seeder ships, over eighteen hundred in total from the six hundred areas, would not have gotten faster. That kind of advancement was done when not worrying about their very survival.

So it would have taken the ships about sixty thousand years to return to where they could have gotten the right seed material to start the seeding over.

And then another sixty thousand years to return to their original areas. But so far, none of the ships had been found anywhere near their original areas. So they had gone somewhere else.

Echo had no idea why they would do that.

At that moment, behind them, a familiar voice said simply, "Permission to resume my duties?"

She and Cole spun around to see JP standing there beside his station, looking worried.

Silence had fallen over the command center as everyone watched.

Echo felt a surge of joy at seeing him again. She stepped up to his level, moved over to him and gave him a massive hug.

When she let him go, Cole, smiling from ear to ear, shook his hand.

"You may resume your duties on one condition," Echo said, staring at the man she and Cole had trusted for decades.

"Anything," JP said.

"No more secrets," Echo said. "We are all Seeders and are all in this together. Agreed?"

"Agreed," JP said.

Echo thought the smile would hurt him. In all their years she had never seen him smile like that before. It made her heart feel light.

Around them the command center broke into cheers. JP was not only well respected, but well loved by everyone. It was wonderful to have him back.

After everything had settled back down, Echo turned to JP. "We are trying to figure out where all the mother ships went. Your culture had to borrow from our culture to start new human seeding, what would these groups have done?"

"They would have left one area human only," JP said. "In our worlds around the center, we had already made our mistake by pulling in Seeders from many seeded planets. When we stopped seeding and then our birthrate experiments failed, and the lifespan dropped, the human cultures we had seeded were too advanced for us to get new material."

"But you had our culture close by, thankfully," Cole said.

"We did," JP said. "Thankfully."

"Did these groups out here know that?" Echo asked.

"No," JP said, shaking his head. "There was no contact. But being this far out, the logical thing would be to depend on one area to remain human seeding."

"Is there any record of any ultimate goal these six hundred groups had?" Cole asked.

"To build a second Center," JP said, "a second home world."

Echo turned back to the big screen. "*Star Trail*, please put up that center location we have all figured would be their destination. Show it with a red dot and show the six hundred plus seeded areas with green dots."

The image appeared on the big screen.

"Now which green dot would be the closest to that red dot?" Cole asked. "Show it brighter."

Echo had an idea and if she was right, this was going to turn out a lot better than anyone could have hoped.

"*Star Trail*," Echo said, "Assuming eighteen hundred mother ships, all seeding at a normal rate for their time, how long would it take to seed every galaxy in a hundred galaxy diameter path to that red dot from that closest green dot?"

"*Approximately three million years,*" Star Trail said. "*That has a variable factor of a hundred thousand years in either direction.*"

"Could we all be that lucky?" JP asked quietly.

"Only one way to find out," Cole said. "Let's talk with the other chairmen and go exploring."

Echo loved that idea.

Especially with JP back at their side.

CHAPTER 20

Cole and Echo stood facing the giant screen as the other chairmen linked in. They had also included Ray and Tacita.

After everyone was linked in, Cole started off. "After consulting with Commander Horshaw, an ancient who we are very happy to have returned to duty with us, we believe we might have an answer."

Cole turned and nodded to JP, who nodded back.

"We believe," Echo said, "that the groups out here would have left one group seeding only humans as a back-up, sort of a seed group if you will."

"The groups here had an intent to build a second major home, a second Center," Cole said. "We believe they would have left the most central group as human seeding."

"And they would have picked the area we have studied as a possible future home," Echo said.

"So if they started from the most central seeded group, the

ones assumed to have humans, and seeded humans all the way in a hundred galaxy diameter area with all eighteen hundred plus mother ships, they would have reached their new home in three million years."

Echo said, "Show the diagram of what we are talking about please?"

An image appeared on the screen with a wide band leading from one green dot to a bright red dot. The wide band was a hundred galaxies wide.

The more Cole thought about this, the more he was convinced it was right and logical. Of course, he had thought that about a number of other theories so far on this mission and all of them had been proven wrong.

On the big screen most of the chairmen were nodding.

"It will take us over three weeks from our location to get to that seeded area. But it would take *Star Ray* only three weeks."

Lisa and Jaden were both nodding.

"I would suggest," Ray said, "That all ships head there. At top speed."

"Why?" Echo asked a fraction of a second before Cole could.

"Because the ancients at the center believe that might have happened as well," Tacita said.

"Since your first discoveries," Ray said, "they have been searching for any records, any information about the overall mission of the different ancient Seeder groups. They always intended, from what can be found, to build civilizations with Seeders only."

"But they wanted to keep one area seeded with humans,"

Tacita said, "to account for what they figured would be a decrease in populations."

"Just as the ancients here discovered," Ray said, "the declining lifespan of Seeders combined with the failed attempts at increasing birthrates would have spelled the doom of the original idea."

"Unless it didn't," Tacita said.

Cole had no idea what she meant by that.

"Either way," Ray said, "that center group will hold a lot of answers."

"Everyone in favor of heading at top speed for that center group?" Cole asked the gathered chairmen.

All nodded.

"Approach with caution and undetected," Ray said.

"See everyone shortly," Cole said, smiling at the rest of the chairmen.

Then he cut the connection.

"*Star Trail*," Echo said. "Are all scout and military ships on board?"

"*Yes*," *Star Trail* said.

"Go to full speed," Cole said. "Let's go see what we can find this time."

This excited him. Again they were moving, looking for answers in the unknown. That was what this ship had been built to do and for one, he was very glad they were back doing it.

CHAPTER 21

Echo had managed to keep herself busy for the past three weeks. This morning both she and Cole had taken their coffee and snack bars instead of breakfast to the command center to watch the feeds coming in from *Star Ray.*

Star Ray was going to be the first ship to enter the area around what they were all hoping would be a fully seeded human culture. It was going to take the rest of the Starburst ships from ten hours up to three more weeks to reach the area. Thankfully, they would be there beside Star Ray in just fifteen hours.

But for now everyone was watching the feeds coming in.

Echo had no idea what might have happened to over one-hundred-and-eighty mother ships if they didn't find humans here.

"We have a galaxy ahead full of terra-formed planets," Jaden said.

Echo and Cole were watching the feeds. Behind them everyone in the command center stood silently, watching as well.

"The data doesn't look right," Cole said, shaking his head.

He glanced back at the command crew. "Get working on what they are sending us."

Everyone went to work instantly. Echo knew that each of them had a specific area of the data they would pore through quickly.

"The worlds appear to be dead," Lisa of *Star Ray* said softly. "Not like we had found before, but destroyed within a fairly recent period of time."

"There are a few human survivors scattered on the planets we are scanning," Jaden said. "Some planets are completely dead. No Gray or Cirrata that we can find at all still surviving."

Echo felt her stomach twist into a knot as *Star Ray* held position on the edge of the galaxy and launched hundreds of scout and military ships, all cloaked. She couldn't believe they were facing more dead human planets like the one she and Cole had worked on all those years before.

As the scout ships went to work quickly, staying shielded and moving in over various planets, the data really started to pour in.

"These were well-advanced human and Gray and Cirrata civilizations," JP said from behind them.

"When did this happen?" Echo asked as the images of cities came flooding in, most still standing but on closer look they were starting to deteriorate.

"When did this happen?" Cole repeated without turning from the big screen. "How long ago?"

"Recent," JP said. "Within one hundred years."

"We're leaving scout ships here and jumping at full speed to the home galaxy," Jaden said from *Star Ray*. "Our ships will track and observe the survivors. We should be at the home galaxy in forty minutes."

"We will drop scout ships and military ships at each galaxy we pass," Lisa said. "We will continue feeds of all incoming data."

Echo just watched the big screen as more and more data started to pour in from the scout ships. Whatever had happened to these planets had happened galaxy wide to every terra-formed and inhabited planet.

Also there was no sign of any ships left in space or any stations left at all. Just floating debris where stations might have been.

And every galaxy *Star Ray* flashed past, the same story emerged. Complete destruction of what had been advanced and clearly stable human, Gray, and Cirrata cultures.

Recent destruction.

And that scared Echo even more than she wanted to admit.

And brought up horrid memories.

CHAPTER 22

ole stood beside Echo in the command center and watched the big screen as *Star Ray* dropped into a holding position outside of the original seeded galaxy and launched hundreds of scout and military ships.

It was clear from first scans that the destruction was the same, only this had been far more recent. Within the last five years on one side of the galaxy. Some planets on the far edge of the galaxy where *Star Ray* had approached still had buildings burning and the data showed that those planets had been just recently attacked. Not more than a week before.

No Gray or Cirrata survivors, but hundreds of thousands of human survivors on almost every planet.

He glanced at Echo, who looked stunned. They both had been hit hard with the years on that destroyed planet trying to help that civilization recover. And that had been a natural disaster. Now, once again, they were looking at a planet with hundreds of thousands of human survivors among the ruins.

It took Cole a moment before he recognized this pattern of destruction across a galaxy. He had seen it before, hundreds of years ago.

The group of humans who had tried a biological experiment and created a race of rats that flooded a galaxy and destroyed everything before moving on. The original group of humans had used devices to move from one side of a galaxy to the other, destroying life on every planet infested with the rats.

So whoever or whatever was doing this was moving from one side of the galaxy to the next and then moving on to the next galaxy in line. And that meant the attackers were close.

And that the attackers were moving slowly.

"Star Trail," Cole said, "please contact the chairmen of *Star Ray*. Private channel."

Lisa and Jaden appeared on the main screen. Both looked white and clearly shocked.

They had not been involved with the war with the rats. They had become chairmen after that, so they might not have seen this pattern at once.

Cole quickly explained the pattern of destruction to them and how it fit from the earlier war, then said simply, "Whatever fleet is doing this, they are still close and headed to the next galaxy. From the looks of their movement, it will take them about four years to cover the distance between the two galaxies."

Beside Cole, Echo was nodding.

Both Lisa and Jaden were also nodding. "We are getting a call from Carey and Matt. *Star Ray*, join them into this conversation."

The worried faces of Carey and Matt appeared.

"Cole has just told us," Jaden said to them, "about this pattern of destruction being clear from the war with the rats."

Carey and Matt both nodded.

"That is the reason we are calling," Carey said. "Whoever did this is still close and moving at far slower speeds than we can move."

Jaden glanced at Lisa. Then he said, *"Star Ray,* launch a hundred military ships on a course for the closest seeded galaxy. And twenty each on courses to other nearby seeded galaxies. Have them stay shielded and report what they find. Do not have them engage or get close to anything they find."

"We'll all be beside you as quickly as we can," Cole said.

"Thank you," Lisa said. "We are going to need a complete conference as we get more information."

At that point they cut the connection.

Cole turned to his command crew. "Get answers, people. We need to know what we are getting into. What kind of weapon caused all this destruction?"

Then he turned back to Echo.

She clearly had something on her mind. He knew that look in her eyes.

"Star Trail," Echo said, "please show on the main screen the locations of each Starburst ship and their path headed toward *Star Ray's* position. Starburst ships in blinking green dots and their path in a green line."

The three-dimensional image of a few million galaxies appeared on the big screen. Nineteen green lines converged on one blinking green light.

"Now show in red the nearest possible seeded galaxies that

might have been seeded on the way to the assumed new home for this group."

Cole watched as *Star Trail* showed a bunch of dots in red spreading away from *Star Ray's* location.

"Five Starburst ships are going close to some of those galaxies," Cole said. "A couple in just a few hours."

Echo nodded. "We're one of them. Exactly what I was thinking might be the case. Let's give Lisa and Jaden thirty minutes for their military ships to find something, then call a full conference."

Cole looked up at the big screen. *"Star Trail,* continue to update the location of the Starburst ships on that image."

"Understood," Star Trail said.

Cole just stared at the big screen. *Star Trail* was going to go within an hour of some possibly seeded galaxies in just five hours. There was no doubt they needed to see what had happened to them.

He wasn't sure he wanted to know.

CHAPTER 23

Echo let the next twenty minutes just drag past as everyone in the Command Center fought to find answers from the data pouring in now from hundreds of *Star Ray's* scout ships.

Then the data from the large military fleet that *Star Ray* had launched came through. *Star Ray's* ships had found the fleet of ships that must have caused the destruction.

Alien ships.

The first image appeared on the main screen and everyone in the Command Center gasped.

Completely alien ships.

Nothing at all like Seeder ships or Cirrata blimp-shaped ships or the Gray saucer-shaped craft.

These alien ships looked more like balls with spikes sticking out from all sides.

And there were a couple thousand of them. Some small, some about half the size of an old Seeder mother ship.

Clearly a fourth race had made it to a stable culture and found the speeds to cross between galaxies.

Echo forced herself to let out the breath she was holding, then from behind her JP said, "We are seeing something on planets in the first galaxy *Star Ray* found."

"Please put it on the big screen," Cole said.

"These are close-up images from a few of the planets destroyed almost a hundred years ago," JP said.

The images were of lush, green continents and some destroyed human cities near the bright blue ocean.

But something was off, very off.

From what Echo could see, it looked like the ground was moving and shifting all along the shoreline.

Then the image zoomed in and it was clear that what she was seeing was some sort of alien-looking bug. A cross between a crab and a spider. Black eyes on four stalks, sharp talons on front feet, four back feet, a hard shell of some sort with black patterns on them.

And there were billions of them in just the images they were seeing and they were all fighting each other, tearing each other apart as they swarmed out of the ocean and covered the land.

"The oceans have a much higher salt and nutrient base than we would have ever allow in terra-formed planets," J.P said. "The oceans have been altered and the oxygen levels of the atmospheres have been lowered as well to a more carbon-heavy combination."

"That's why almost no humans are left alive on these early destroyed planets," Cole said.

"With those creatures coming out of the oceans like that,"

Echo said, "the survivors or any animals on that planet won't last much longer anyway."

"The human survivors need to be evacuated," Cole said.

Echo nodded. From the reports coming in, *Star Ray* already had ships getting ready to do just that.

Were the swarming creatures the aliens? If so, what was happening?

Then Cole answered her unasked question with a statement that sent chills down her spine.

"Oh, shit," Cole said. "The aliens are seeding."

The deathly silence in the Command Center felt heavy with Cole's statement.

The images on the big screen were horrific. It looked almost like one creature swallowing up an entire planet.

"*Star Trail*," Echo said, "put the image of the map of Starburst ships and their locations back on the screen."

Cole nodded and turned around and thanked JP with a nod.

Echo couldn't get the images out of her mind. They had always known they might find aliens in all the billions of galaxies that would not be compatible in any fashion with humans. They had actually found many younger civilizations that had been spider or crab-like. But none of those had made it out of their own galaxy or even come close.

So this was clearly something that wasn't completely unexpected, except for the part of attacking advanced human and Gray and Cirrata cultures and wiping them out.

Cultures without defenses.

Seeded cultures usually cleared out their military as they advanced and stabilized. It had only been the war with the rats that had caused Seeders to bring back the military side of things in their ships. And right now Echo was very glad they had.

Very, very glad.

CHAPTER 24

C ole couldn't believe what he had seen on those planets. Clearly the aliens had changed the oceans in some way and left eggs or some sort of device to create millions of aliens to swarm over the land.

He had no idea if those swarms looked like the aliens in the ships, but he was betting they did.

They scared him at a base level. He had seen images of many alien races over the years. Some had repulsed him, some scared him. These scared him more than any others had.

And something about the way they swarmed over everything and fought each other twisted his stomach.

"The Chairmen of the Star Ray are asking for a conference call," Star Trail said.

"Link us in," Echo said.

Cole took a deep breath and made himself calm down as much as possible.

A moment later the main screen cleared to show the other nineteen Starburst ships' chairmen and Ray and Tacita.

"We have only found the one fleet," Jaden said.

Cole was very relieved to hear that.

"The alien fleet is traveling at trans-tunnel twelve," Lisa said, "and will reach the next galaxy in just under four years. We have sent ships ahead and they will be reporting on the state of the next galaxy in the fleet's path within minutes."

Echo nodded, as did numbers of other chairmen on the big screen conference. They all liked the news that the alien ships were slow. That bought them time to study and make decisions.

"We believe we need to do a number of things almost at once," Jaden said.

Beside Jaden, Lisa nodded. "First, we need to backtrack and see where this alien fleet originated. That mission is already launched with three hundred military ships and three hundred scout ships."

"Second," Jaden said, "we need to scout all the possible surrounding galaxies that might have human cultures and check on their status."

"We understand that five of your ships will be approaching some possible seeded galaxies shortly," Lisa said. "We suggest you move toward those galaxies and explore as widely as you can while still making good speed. Watch for any possible alien home galaxy."

"Our military ships have the alien fleet surrounded completely and are staying shielded," Jaden said. "The aliens do not know we are there. We could stop them at a moment's notice, destroy them completely, but we feel we should study them as much as possible before taking any action."

Cole found himself nodding to that, as were most of the other chairmen.

"Third, we need to develop a map of exactly which human cultures are in this area," Lisa said, "how old they are, and where these aliens have seeded. It is clear they are seeding in the first destroyed human galaxies we came across. We will assume that seeding is their mission until other evidence supports a different theory."

"Then lastly," Jaden said, "we may need to send ahead a few ships toward the area we believe holds the new home of these human cultures. We need to see if any damage has happened in those areas."

"Anyone have any questions or suggestions?"

Carey of *Star Fall* said, "I do. We need to also look for evidence that this alien culture was human, Gray, or Cirrata created."

Cole again found himself nodding. Considering that many of them had fought a centuries-long war because of a human-created plague culture, that made complete sense.

"Agreed," Jaden said. "Ray and Tacita, we will need to have you in contact and updating the ancients in the Center on this. Have them searching their databases for anything in history like what we are seeing."

"We will do so," Tacita said.

"Another conference in six hours unless a major discovery happens ahead of then," Jaden said.

With that the conference ended.

Cole let out a breath he didn't realize he was holding. He

was very happy that Lisa and Jaden had taken complete control of the situation. So now it was up to him and Echo and the crew of *Star Trail* to see what they could find over the next few hours in possible human-seeded galaxies.

He and Echo and JP, along with *Star Trail*, worked for the next fifteen minutes on which galaxies to go to first. They decided to set a course where they could scan hundreds of galaxies while still moving at full speed toward a possible edge of human seeded space.

One hour later they found what Cole was hoping against hope they would not find.

An alien galaxy.

And not built in the remains of a human galaxy, but all on its own.

CHAPTER 25

Echo just stared at the image of the spiral galaxy full of alien planets on the large screen. The idea of a complete alien galaxy just gave her shudders. The scene of the aliens swarming over the beaches and fighting had scared her at a very deep level. Far more than she wanted to admit to herself or to Cole.

"*Star Trail*, drop out of trans-tunnel near the galaxy," Cole said. "Make sure we and all scout and military ships are completely shielded. Send two hundred of both types of ship throughout the alien galaxy to gather up-close data."

Echo added, "Also send as many groups of fifty scout and military ships as needed ahead on our course to scout the next galaxies along our intended path."

"*Holding position*," Star Trail said. "*Ships launching.*"

From what Echo could tell from the data starting to pour in, the galaxy was a fully-formed, galaxy-wide alien culture in a medium-sized spiral galaxy about the same size as the Milky

Way. Millions of alien ships of all sizes were in flight between systems.

More and more information started to pour in almost immediately as the scout and military ships flashed to different points of the galaxy.

The alien culture seemed to exist half on the land and half in the seas on Earth-like planets around yellow stars. They clearly liked the same basic kinds of planets as humans, Gray, and Cirrata did.

Echo watched as the first images of the aliens appeared on the screen. They had the features of spiders combined with crabs, just larger versions of the ones swarming over those planets that *Star Ray* had found.

They were all black and gray, with hard shells and there seemed no way to tell them apart, which Echo knew meant nothing.

Again she barely contained a shudder.

"They are moving like ants," Cole said, watching one image coming in from what seemed to be a large city, but looked more like a giant pile of hardened dirt towering above the shore of an ocean.

"Hive mind?" Echo asked, now really worried. No alien culture that functioned as a hive mind that she had ever studied had managed to get off of their own planet. Let alone spread over a galaxy and to other galaxies.

As the next few minutes passed quickly and data poured in, the scout ships started to report that they had found the center of each planet, what appeared to be the main city on each planet.

And under the city was a vast network of partially flooded

tunnels all leading to one massive creature in a huge underground cavern.

"Each planet has a queen," Cole said, his voice soft.

Echo was thinking the exact same thing, but they needed to be careful.

"We can't assume anything in an alien culture," Echo said. "We need to show this to the other chairmen and give the scientists time to look at all this data."

Cole nodded. "*Star Trail*, contact the other Starburst ship chairmen and Ray and Tacita. On the main screen please."

A moment later the faces of the other chairmen appeared. All of them looked very worried.

"We found an alien galaxy," Cole said. "*Star Trail*, send all Starburst ships and Chairmen Ray and Tacita the images we are getting from our scout ships.

"We believe we have also found what appears to be a queen of some sort on each planet," Echo said. "At first glance, the aliens seem to move as if controlled by a hive mind."

At that moment behind her JP said, "Scout ships reporting in from ahead."

Cole nodded. "Put those reports in the corner of the screen please, for everyone to see."

Echo glanced at the reports coming in from the scout ships they had sent ahead to other galaxies. Now she felt like she wanted to just sit down and put her head between her knees.

"Correction," she said. "We have found at least ten alien galaxies so far. None of which were built in the remains of a human-seeded culture."

"We are continuing the search for more," Cole said.

The stunned look on the other chairmen's faces was enough to tell the entire story.

Echo felt the same way exactly. None of them had any idea what to do next.

She wasn't sure there was anything they could do except protect the next human galaxy.

SECTION FIVE

THE ALIENS

CHAPTER 26

For a moment the conference was silent as everyone studied the data being sent by *Star Trail* to them. Cole did the same, stunned at the extent of the wide alien culture they were just beginning to find.

"We will send ships from here and determine the extent of the alien spread through the galaxies close to this one," Echo said to the other chairmen.

Cole nodded. That was going to be critical information.

"The ancients, the Gray, and the Cirrata," Ray said, "have no knowledge of such a culture existing, but they do not believe such a culture would be unusual."

"We are going to need to try to talk with these new aliens at some point," Tacita said. "So please keep that in mind. We will be studying here how to do so."

Cole was actually shocked at that idea, but Ray and a few other chairmen on the screen were nodding.

"The ancients," Ray said, "believe it is possible the aliens didn't even understand the human and Gray and Cirrata cultures on those planets."

Cole found that almost impossible to imagine, yet this was a completely alien culture.

"Hive mind," Tacita said, nodding. "If you are correct in that assumption, the aliens in the ships would only be workers without any ability to judge or think in a creative fashion."

"Just following orders," Ray said. "And thus not be able to recognize another culture."

All the chairmen were nodding now.

"So we need a vast amount of information yet," Cole said.

"Stay shielded everyone," Echo said. "We will report back as soon as we have a clearer image of the extent of this culture or during the next meeting *Star Ray* has set."

At that Echo cut the conference call and turned to look at Cole.

Cole reached over and hugged her with one arm, turning them both to face JP.

He was looking as shocked as Cole was feeling. And the silence in the command center spoke volumes on how everyone was feeling.

"Well," Cole said to everyone. "We joined onto this Starburst project to go explore and find stuff. Seems we have found a lot of stuff."

A couple of the crew laughed and JP just shook his head, smiling.

"Now let's figure out a way to quickly find the extent of this alien culture's spread."

"*Star Trail*," Echo said, turning back to face the big screen.

"Show us a three-dimensional image of a few thousand galaxies surrounding this galaxy."

The image appeared.

"Mark this galaxy red and all other known alien galaxies red," Cole said. "Adjust the scale to include the alien seeded galaxies *Star Ray* has found. And put in a blinking blue dot the location of the alien fleet."

To Cole the pattern was instantly clear. From the galaxy where they were, there was a clear path to the fleet.

"*Star Trail*," Cole said, "Show a dotted straight line from this galaxy to the alien fleet."

The line appeared. Beside Cole, Echo nodded.

"*Star Trail*," Echo said, "Extend that line back in the opposite direction from this galaxy, then show our path approaching this galaxy in an orange line."

"We came in sideways on this line of seeding," Cole said. "We have to go back along that line to see how far it goes."

"And if this is a hive mind at work," Echo said, "a galaxy-spanning hive mind, we need to find that original home with the original queen."

"And then what?" JP asked from behind them.

Cole could only shake his head. He had no idea.

None at all.

CHAPTER 27

Echo spent some time talking with Cole about sending scout ships back, or if they should take *Star Trail* back along the clear trail of alien seeded galaxies. They really needed to find where these aliens all started.

Finally they decided that *Star Ray* would have enough help shortly from all the other Starburst ships headed there. *Star Trail* needed to find the start of this race, the alien home world. So they informed *Star Ray* to pull back the ships they had back-tracking.

Then they sent the image of the line of seeding to all the chairmen.

Echo was starting to think that if this alien race really was a hive mind, there just might be one major queen that controlled it all.

"*Star Trail*," Cole said, after he and Echo made sure all scout and military ships were accounted for and most were back on board, "follow along that extended line at full speed, scanning galaxies as we pass."

"Stop when you no longer find an alien-seeded galaxy," Echo said. "And show our path on the screen."

"Engaging full trans-tunnel drive," Star Trail said.

Echo watched as dozens and dozens of galaxies flashed past, all with alien cultures.

Then, almost as quickly as it started, *Star Trail* dropped out of trans-tunnel drive.

"Scanning a dozen galaxies ahead shows no sign of alien culture," Star Trail said.

"Return to the edge of the last alien galaxy," Cole said.

"Launch three hundred scout ships with military escorts to scout the galaxy," Echo said, "and another four hundred scout ships to scan all surrounding galaxies in groups of twenty."

A moment later *Star Trail* said, *"Near the last alien galaxy. Launching scout and military ships."*

"Please show the path on the large screen with a dotted line from this galaxy to the alien fleet," Cole said.

Echo watched as the image appeared. "How many alien galaxies are along that path?"

"From two-hundred-and-sixty confirmed to five-hundred-and-ten possible," Star Trail said, *"depending on the results of galaxies along that line that have not been scanned."*

Echo stood beside Cole as both of them studied the data coming in from the scout ships. As with the previous galaxy, every planet seemed to have a queen center.

"Star Trail, is it possible to determine when this galaxy was settled by the aliens?" Cole asked.

"Approximately one-point-six million years ago," Star Trail said.

"With a possible variation of two hundred thousand years in either direction."

"The Seeders were in this area of space first," Echo said, shocked at that information.

"Chances are they never got this far away from their home galaxy in this direction," Cole said. "At their speeds this galaxy and the first seeded human galaxy were over three hundred years travel time apart. No reason to come this way."

"And they were headed with seeding in the other direction," Echo said.

Now she understood that the human culture and the alien culture being this close had just been a bad piece of luck, and that the aliens seeding in the direction of the human galaxies had also just been a very bad piece of luck.

"Star Trail," Cole said, "is this is the oldest alien galaxy?"

"Of the ones scanned, yes, this is the oldest," Star Trail said.

"So now we need to find the original home world," Echo said.

The galaxy was a standard spiral galaxy, not large but not small either. It would have over a billion possible planets around yellow stars. Echo had no idea how they were going to narrow that down to find one home alien world.

But at least they had found the alien home galaxy.

That was a start.

CHAPTER 28

Cole was about to suggest to Echo that they call a conference when *Star Trail* informed them that Lisa and Jaden were calling a conference.

All nineteen Starburst ship's chairmen appeared on the large screen along with Ray and Tacita.

"We have some good news to report," Jaden said, starting right off. "The galaxy the alien ships are headed toward has a healthy and advanced human culture in it. No damage there or any sign any alien ship has even approached that galaxy."

"And the human populations of the billion-plus planets," Lisa said, "seem to have no idea they are within years of being destroyed."

Cole was very happy to hear all that.

Very happy and very relieved.

"We have found no other alien cultures off the line of seeding they are clearly traveling," Jaden said.

"Even better news," Lisa said. "Ancient-seeded human cultures have spread out as we had expected in a band of about fifty galaxies wide and the band seems to be moving in the direction of where we assume the center home worlds of this group of Seeders would be."

"So we have a pretty good idea what happened to all the mother ships," Jaden said. "They just kept on seeding."

"There seems to be no communication at all between the human galaxies," Lisa said. "Thus they would have no idea about the destruction that has happened or the threat."

Cole understood that. Seeded human galaxies tended to not expand outside of their own galaxy, even though they had the speed to do so with long missions. It was the Seeders, because of the last war, that had set up the breadcrumb networks both with Starburst ships and mother ships, but also between galaxies recently seeded. The idea was to try to pull the galaxy-wide cultures together.

It would be many centuries before the results of that would be clear, although faster ship speeds would certainly help that as well.

As Jaden paused, Echo said to the chairmen, "It appears we have found the original alien galaxy. We have not found their original home planet yet and the main queen, but given time we believe we can."

Cole told everyone the amount of time the aliens had been in existence and sent them all an updated map of the seeding trail of the aliens. "We have scout ships out making sure no other seeding lines were done by the aliens."

"This is all good news," Ray said, nodding.

"We will next need to figure out," Tacita said, "how the queens are communicating with the workers, if this actually is a hive mind culture. That needs to be the next priority."

"Agreed," Jaden said.

Cole nodded, as did Echo beside him and the other chairmen on the screen.

But then Matt from Starburst ship *Star Fall* said, "I think there may be more going on than we are seeing."

Beside him Carey nodded. Cole could tell they both looked very, very worried.

"Some of you chairmen," Matt said, "lived for a time on a planet in the Milky Way Galaxy that had a population destroyed by a radiation burst from space. That planet was our home planet."

Cole glanced at Echo who had gone a little white. They had spent six years there trying to help out the rebirth of that society, living and dealing with the dead. It had been a tough six years for both of them.

"We have been studying the data coming in from the planets just attacked by the aliens," Carey said. "There are survivors, but no dead."

"Those cities had millions of people in them and there isn't one sign that anyone in those cities died," Matt said.

"It was as if almost all of the population wasn't there," Carey said, "when the aliens arrived and started getting the planet ready for their seeding."

"Where could they have gone?" Ray asked.

The exact question that Cole was thinking. And he bet the same question that every chairman was asking.

Carey and Matt both shook their heads.

"The population of the planets seemed to be advanced and stabilized at around three billion per planet," Matt said. "We estimate around a billion human planets in the last galaxy."

Cole couldn't even do the math on that number of people, couldn't imagine it. And he really didn't want to think about that many people dying.

Silence over the large screen.

Finally it was Ray who said simply, "We all have a lot of work to do. Map out that entire area of space, make sure on everything, and see if you can find out what happened to all those people."

Tacita nodded and then cut their connection.

"Tomorrow morning at ten for another conference," Lisa said.

With that the conference ended.

Echo nodded to Cole and turned to face their command crew. "Miss no detail, people. We need to find that original alien home world and understand how this alien culture works."

"*Star Trail*," Cole said. "I want a search pattern in a one-hundred-galaxy radius of this galaxy completed quickly. Scout and military ships in bands of twenty each. Set it up and launch the ships as needed."

"That's going to be a lot of information coming in," Echo said to the command crew. "Set up teams to analyze every bit and fit it together."

Cole watched as his fantastic command crew nodded and set to work.

Echo turned back to him. "Come with me."

And a moment later they had jumped to their apartment.

"We need food," Echo said, moving to the kitchen area.

At that moment Cole realized he was hungry. And he couldn't even remember what meal they had had last.

Or even what time it was.

CHAPTER 29

Echo cooked them some simple hamburgers with fries and made them both a chocolate milkshake. Their three orange-and-white cats sort of watched from the edge of the living room, more surprised at the odd schedule than anything else.

While she cooked, Cole just sat at the dining table, clearly deep in thought. They often sat together, not talking.

Finally, as they were eating, she brought up what Carey and Matt had been talking about.

It had bothered Echo more than she wanted to admit and she needed to talk about it. Those years going into homes of the dead had made her understand just how unbelievably precious human life was.

And how fragile.

"What do you think happened to all those people on all those planets?" Echo asked. "Or their bodies? You think the aliens are to blame?"

Cole shook his head and kept eating, but she could tell the idea had bothered him as well.

She couldn't imagine how this was bothering Matt and Carey and a few of the other chairmen of Starburst ships who had spent time in the rescue there or in the rebuilding.

She knew that Jaden and Lisa were waiting for a few other Starburst ships to arrive before starting rescue operations of the surviving humans. But that would take another week or so. And Echo was very glad she and Cole were not involved in that kind of planning.

"Something purposeful had to have happened to them," Cole said after a moment. "On that planet in the Milky Way, over a million people had survived worldwide from a nasty natural disaster. But that left billions and billions dead, scattered everywhere. You don't just hide that many bodies in a few years."

"But where did they go then?" Echo asked, trying to wrap her mind around doing something with billions of people from a planet and then doing that on a billion planets.

Cole shook his head, again with the haunted look in his eyes. "The only logical conclusion is that the alien fleet did something to them. A weapon of some sort that dissolved them or broke the bodies down into a dust and only a few survived that."

Echo had come up with the same thought. But that would argue against the idea that the aliens might not even have noticed the civilizations on the planets they were preparing to seed.

"We need to find this alien home planet," Echo said, "and

figure out what kind of weapons these aliens have and if we are in danger as well."

Cole nodded. "Not at all convinced our screens would protect us from something like that."

"I'm not convinced they don't know we are here," Echo said.

"Yeah," Cole said, "had that same thought."

The idea that their shields couldn't protect them scared Echo more than she wanted to admit.

Far, far more.

With that they both finished their meals.

Then Cole made them both large cups of coffee and jumped back to the command center while Echo gave their cats a treat and made sure their water supply was full.

Then she joined him, her coffee mug in hand, focused on finding the answer to what had happened to billions and billions of humans.

Something clearly had happened to them. She needed to know what had happened.

But she just wasn't sure she really wanted to know.

CHAPTER 30

C ole was surprised that the next two weeks became a form of routine. He never would have thought it could, but it did.

Neither he nor Echo had gone back to exercising yet, so every morning after about six hours sleep and a quick breakfast, they found themselves in the command center.

That's where they both were now, with large cups of coffee, studying all the data coming over the large screen in front of them.

Twice a day they had conference calls with the other chairmen.

Every hour he and Echo got summary reports from all the areas of data coming in from the command crew.

They had yet to discover the original alien home world, but they felt they were narrowing it down.

The galaxies in a radius around this galaxy held no

171

surprises at all and all scout ships not working inside the alien galaxy were now back on board.

The information about the aliens had been slowly growing. They were clearly a hive mind culture with one queen.

The aggressive nature that was evident when the aliens were young and coming out of the ocean was not evident at all with the adults of the race. Cole was very happy to hear that.

There seemed, at least from any human viewpoints, to not be any weapons or defenses on any of the planets.

The alien fleet seemed to have no weapons of any nature and beyond simple shields against dust and small particles, the alien ships seemed to have no defensive shields either.

Their trans-tunnel drives seemed to be basic and clearly alien-designed. No sign of human or Gray or Cirrata designs in the slightest.

And there was still no evidence at all on how the aliens communicated.

There were now six of the twenty Starburst ships with *Star Ray* and the others would be arriving over the next two weeks. The more ships that arrived in the area, the more comfortable Cole felt.

That was a lot of people working on the same problems and a lot of military might if needed.

The first conference call with the other chairmen was just over a half hour away when behind Cole, JP said, "We found it. We found the original planet and maybe the main queen."

"Details on the big screen," Echo said.

Cole could see that the original alien planet was located near the edge of the galaxy in one spiral arm. It orbited in a standard orbit that allowed for water and oxygen and life to survive around a middle-aged yellow sun.

A massive alien city that looked more like a giant mountain filled the center of one large continent. And from all the scans the scout ships had taken, the largest living creature ever imagined filled the inside of that mountain.

"That queen is bigger than this ship," Echo said, her voice showing shock. "How is that possible?"

"From what we can tell," JP said, "It's far over a million years old as well."

Cole couldn't even grasp what he was seeing. The Gray, the Cirrata, and the humans were all small creatures with similar characteristics, even though very different.

But a creature larger than *Star Trail* and that old was truly alien in nature.

Cole was just shaking his head. Now what do they do?

"You are being contacted by the Sun Hawk chairmen," Star Trail said.

Echo glanced at Cole, a puzzled look on her face.

It took Cole a moment before the name sank in.

Sun Hawk was one of the Seeder mother ships they had been searching for from the first seeded area they had found.

What in the world were they doing here?

"Please, *Star Trail*," Cole said, "put them through on the big screen."

Behind them the command center went dead silent.

On the main screen was a man with a balding head and white hair and fairly dark skin. Beside him stood a woman with long gray hair, almost as long as Ray's, and pure white skin. Both of them looked like they were wearing comfortable shirts and jeans.

And both were smiling.

Behind them was what looked to be a massive command center, one level higher and about twice the size of the *Star Trail* command center. It was staffed by well over a hundred humans of various sizes and shapes and dress.

Except for the size of the command center, it looked pretty standard Seeder model.

"Chairmen Guinn and Lemmon," the man said, nodding. "It is an honor to meet you."

"We are Chairmen Sky Mead and Lennox Summerlin of *Sun Hawk*. Please call us Sky and Lennox."

Cole managed to open his mouth, but nothing came out.

Echo managed a little more.

"Please call us Echo and Cole," she said. "A pleasure and a vast surprise to meet you, to say the least."

Both smiled. "We have been following you for a while now and watching your movements and *Star Ray's* movements as well," Sky said. "We hoped to hold off contacting you for a little longer but since you have found the Karinos' home world, we felt it was critical we do so now."

Cole again was almost too stunned to talk. Then he asked simply, "How long have you been watching us?"

Sky glanced at Lennox and he shrugged. "Honestly, we have had scout ships around all the Starburst ships since you all arrived in our old home areas of space. A very impressive mission to discover what happened to all of us."

"Commendable," Sky said.

"Yes, very much so," Lennox said.

"We need to ask you a favor," Sky said, getting serious before Cole or Echo could even say a word about what they had just heard.

"We need to ask you to withdraw your scout ships from around the Karinos' home planet and this galaxy before the great queen discovers you," Sky said.

Cole assumed she meant the massive queen they had just found, but they went on before he could ask.

"We have, as all Seeders have had, a very aggressive non-intervention and non-contact policy about alien races," Lennox said. "So if you don't mind, would you withdraw all your scout and military ships and we can move away from this galaxy a short distance and talk."

Echo glanced at Cole.

At this moment in time he was too shocked to even have any objection. The scout ships could always return if needed. He wasn't sure if they were being played in some fashion or another, but pulling in the scout and military ships wouldn't make much of a difference.

"*Star Trail*," Cole said, "please issue an emergency recall of all ships around this galaxy and inform us when all ships are back on board."

"Thank you," Sky said, nodding.

"*Sun Hawk*," Lennox said, "please send *Star Trail* a destination a number of galaxies away from any Karinos-seeded galaxies."

"*Destination confirmed,*" Star Trail said.

"We will talk there," Lennox said, smiling. "In one hour."

"We assume you have a lot of questions to ask and we have some answers we can give you," Sky said.

175

With that they vanished.

"Star Trail," Cole said, "any sign of any human Seeder ship in our area?"

"No," Star Trail said simply.

"Any idea where that transmission originated?" Cole asked.

"No," Star Trail again said, simply.

Cole glanced at Echo who was looking puzzled and shocked.

"Any bets we were just played by the alien queen?" Cole asked.

"No bets at all," Echo said.

SECTION SIX

THE REAL SURPRISE

CHAPTER 31

E cho just felt shocked.

And scared out of her mind. What kind of trap were they going to go into?

She and Cole had spent the next ten minutes studying all the data *Star Trail* had about the communication. It had been real, of that there was no doubt.

It had been recorded by *Star Trail*. But it hadn't come from anywhere in particular.

Star Trail said that it had been blocked completely with contact with *Sun Hawk,* if there really was a ship there.

"We need to tell the other chairmen what just happened," Cole finally said.

Echo agreed. At least if they were walking into a trap, the other chairmen would know what was happening.

As the chairmen finished coming onto the screen just slightly ahead of the regular meeting, Echo started off the news.

179

"First off, we found the alien home world," she said.

"But that is not why we called this meeting slightly early," Cole said. "*Star Trail*, play them the supposed meeting we had with the chairmen of the *Sun Hawk* within minutes of discovering the alien home world."

"*Sun Hawk?*" Ray asked, clearly stunned.

The rest of the chairmen's faces were just as stunned. It would have been funny if it wasn't so serious.

At that moment the meeting was starting to play for the chairmen. She and Cole could see all the faces of the other chairmen and Ray and Tacita's faces as well.

When Sky and Lennox appeared on the screen, both Ray and Tacita damn near burst into tears. Tacita actually moved backwards and sat down.

Echo always considered Tacita to be one of the toughest women she had ever met, so something about seeing images of Sky and Lennox had shaken her to her core.

What in the world would do that?

After the recording finished, Cole said, "All of our ships are coming on board now and will be in place in the next five minutes. The meeting point designated is less than ten minutes away."

"We are not sure if that was the alien queen staging that or if by some chance that was actually the chairmen of *Sun Hawk*," Cole said.

"If it was *Sun Hawk*," Echo said, "they have advanced farther than we have in technology and are at least as fast in travel speed."

"Those were two real people," Tacita said, her voice firm

and now back under control. She had stood again as the recording of the meeting had ended.

"We know them very well from the first few seeding missions outside our first galaxy," Tacita said.

"We saw their names on the lists after all these years for the first time when we got the ancient's names with the seeding missions," Ray said. "We did not expect them to still be alive."

"They might not be," Cole said. "This alien culture must have a powerful form of telepathy to communicate from planet to planet and galaxy to galaxy. We have no idea what that kind of power is capable of doing."

Ray and Tacita nodded.

"Whatever or whoever is behind this," Echo said, "they effectively got us to remove our scout and military ships from that galaxy for the moment."

"So we are going to go find out who they really are and if they even exist," Cole said.

"*Star Trail*," Echo said, "please set up a constant feed to all the other Starburst ships and Ray and Tacita of our movements and communications."

With that, Cole cut the conference and he and Echo turned to the command crew. "Everyone stay alert. Scan everything and if you see something off report it instantly."

The silent command crew nodded.

"*Star Trail*, are all ships on board?" Echo asked.

"*The last will be on board in thirty seconds,*" *Star Trail* said.

"At that point jump us to the designated meeting location," Cole said. "Full screens and full speed. Keep all military ships on high alert and ready to launch."

"On the main screen please scan ahead for anything waiting for us at that location," Echo said.

"Entering trans-tunnel drive now," Star Trail said.

The main screen showed nothing at the designation point.

The distance was a full ten minutes away and Echo watched the scans of the empty passing galaxies as they flashed past.

Nothing.

That was the longest ten minutes Echo ever experienced.

Twice she had to force herself to breathe.

And not one word was spoken the entire time in the command center.

Not one.

CHAPTER 32

Destination point. Dropping out of trans-tunnel drive," Star Trail said.

"Hold position," Cole said.

The screen in front of them showed nothing. They were a short distance away from a small spiral galaxy that showed no life at all. This was empty space by any definition.

Cole glanced around at JP who just shook his head.

Nothing at all.

Finally, *Star Trail* said, *"We are being hailed by Sun Hawk."*

"Please, on screen," Cole said. "And make sure this is streaming to all other Starburst ships."

If they were going to make a huge mistake here, he wanted to make sure none of the other Starburst ships would make the same one in the future.

"Thank you for believing us and pulling your scout ships," Lennox said as the two chairmen came on the screen.

Both Sky and Lennox were smiling. Cole could see that both

actually showed a poise that must have come with age. Clearly these two were almost as old as Ray and Tacita. And Sky's long gray hair looked similar to Ray's long gray hair.

"We do not think that the Karinos queen felt any disturbance," Sky said.

Lennox nodded. "We are being very, very careful and studying the Karinos to figure out how or if we should ever contact them."

Cole understood that completely.

"So you promised us some answers," Echo said a moment before Cole could.

He was just stunned again at the two ancients facing him on the screen. They looked so normal and relaxed.

"And we will answer as honestly as we can," Lennox said, continuing to smile.

"Where exactly are you?" Echo said. "You can clearly see us but we can't seem to see you."

"We actually can't see you in any real fashion," Sky said. "We have just learned to trace shielded ships is all. As for where we are, we are very near you. *Sun Hawk*, please drop all screens except those used to protect the ship from debris."

A moment later, filling the screen, a massive ship in the standard Seeder bird shape shimmered into being. It looked sleek, yet massive, like a bird coasting in flight.

But to Cole something felt off about it.

It looked like a more advanced Seeder ship. Same standard shape, everything.

Information about the ship scrolled up the side of the big screen and suddenly Cole understood what felt off about the ship they were looking at.

It was a hundred times, if not more, larger than *Star Trail*.

Sun Hawk was so big, it could hold all twenty of the Starburst ships inside it and not even strain.

"Wow," Echo said, "*Sun Hawk* is a very large and beautiful ship."

"Thank you," Sky said, smiling. "We think so."

"*Star Trail*," Cole said, "please drop our visual and sensory screens, only leaving up the screens necessary for our protection."

Lennox nodded and smiled. "Seeder ships never do seem to change in look, do they?"

"Just size it seems," Cole said, smiling back. "How many souls do you have on board?"

"About two-hundred-million total of crew and families, plus military and scout ship crews and families," Sky said.

"Can I ask speed?" Cole asked.

"Not much faster than you appear to be," Lennox said. "Trans-tunnel forty-eight."

"Are you a Seeder ship?" Echo asked.

"No," Sky said. "At the moment we are one of a thousand ships this size that are being used to rescue humans from the planets in the way of the Karinos seeding. We have three more galaxies to deal with before the Karinos seeding ships move past settled human space and into empty galaxies."

So that was what had happened to the populations of those planets in that last galaxy. They had all been relocated.

"The Gray have about seven-hundred rescue ships," Sky said, "and the Cirrata have five hundred. Luckily, the other two alien races that make up our confederation, the Procyon and the Portia are not living on these early seeded planets."

"You have five races working together?" Echo asked.

"We have explored a great deal of space," Lennox said. "It seems six races that we know about have managed to escape the confines of their galaxies and gone exploring. Five live peacefully together on seeded planets in billions of galaxies and the Karinos are the sixth. To be honest, we have not yet figured out how to approach the Karinos."

"So they do not know you are here on these planets they are destroying?"

"No," Sky said. "At least as far as we know."

"Which is why we have these ships to evacuate populations," Lennox said. "We're starting on the next galaxy in line in a few weeks. We have been seeding and building their new home worlds now for a few thousand years. We started when we discovered the Karinos and the track they were seeding."

"A massive project," Echo said and Cole nodded.

At that moment *Star Trail* said only to Cole and Echo, *"Ray and Tacita would like to join the conversation."*

Echo glanced at Cole. "Why not?"

Echo smiled and turned back to address Lennox and Sky. "We would like to bring in two chairmen to this conversation that say they used to know you. If you don't mind."

"Our pleasure," Lennox said.

Sky looked puzzled.

"Star Trail, please add Chairmen Ray and Tacita to the conversation," Cole said.

Both Lennox and Sky jerked at the mention of those two names.

Then, as the two smiling faces of Ray and Tacita came on the screen, Sky stepped forward.

"Mom? Dad?" Sky asked, her voice not much more than a whisper.

Ray and Tacita just nodded, smiling the largest smiles Cole could ever imagine possible.

All he could do was stare at all four of them.

CHAPTER 33

E cho watched the family reunion clearly millions of years overdue.

After a short time, Sky asked where Ray and Tacita were. When Tacita told them they were in their original seeded area, Sky was very disappointed.

Echo would have been as well. But then Ray told Sky and Lennox they were on their way and would be there in two days.

That news shocked Sky and Lennox, so Ray had to explain the breadcrumb stations to them.

"We will be on our way shortly," Tacita said.

"We are so excited to see you again," Ray said.

With that Ray and Tacita cut out of the conversation, leaving Echo and Cole again facing the smiling faces of Sky and Lennox.

"Well, that was a surprise," Lennox said.

"To all of us as well," Cole said, laughing.

"You didn't know?" Sky asked.

"Ray and Tacita have been the leading figures for millions of years," Cole said, "in hundreds of thousands of galaxy seeding. They don't talk much."

Both Sky and Lennox laughed. "Yeah, that we remember as well."

"So what can our twenty Starburst ships do to help?" Echo asked, changing the subject.

"Besides stay out of the way," Cole said.

"Actually," Lennox said, "we were hoping you would offer."

"We need to focus on getting the main populations of over a billion planets to their new homes," Sky said.

Cole knew exactly where they were going. "You need help with the ones that wouldn't leave originally, but now might want to?"

"Exactly," Lennox said. "We have managed to get most of the stragglers off the planets where the Karinos are hatching their first wave."

"But not all," Cole said. "We were getting ready to try to help the remaining off some of those planets."

"We do not force anyone to leave their home," Sky said. "But seeing those Karinos hatchlings swarming the beaches might change some minds."

"It would change mine," Echo said.

"Let us talk with the other chairmen and get back with you," Cole said.

"And we will hold here until Ray and Tacita arrive through the breadcrumb network we have left behind us," Echo said, smiling.

"We will hold as well," Lennox said, nodding.

"And thank you for the wonderful surprise," Sky said.

"Wish we would have planned it," Echo said, smiling.

With that, the conversation ended.

"Star Trail," Cole said, "put on the main screen all the chairmen of the Starburst ships."

He had a hunch he knew how this was going to go. He couldn't imagine any of them not wanting to help.

But it was sure fun to see the faces appear on the screen laughing and smiling.

And behind every couple was a command center full of smiling faces as well.

It seems the mission they had all set out to do, find the ancients, was a complete success.

And Cole had to admit, that felt wonderful.

EPILOGUE

Echo stood beside Cole in the command center and watched on the big screen as the ground teams on dozens and dozens of planets worked to find humans still remaining. The images were of ruined buildings and dust covering everything. A horrid reminder of the six years on a planet she wished she could forget.

The new images were already starting to give her nightmares.

The two weeks since their first meeting with Lennox and Sky had gone quickly. All of the chairmen of the Starburst ships had agreed without discussion to try to save as many of the stragglers as possible.

All the Starburst ships had spent part of the two weeks setting up quarters for all the possible new arrivals. And getting to know Lennox and Sky's culture and the history of the last four million years for all these seeded groups.

It seemed that all but one of the groups had started the

process to genetically alter entire populations to be born as Seeders.

But by the time it became clear that the lifespan of the new Seeders had fallen, the process was irreversible and the birthrate couldn't be increased. No amount of work could increase the birthrate of the Seeders and they all knew they were doomed.

So at a half million years and with sharply reduced and dwindling populations in each galaxy, they built new Seeder mother ships and used them as jumping points, their own bread-crumb trail, to get the populations to new worlds near the one seeded group that hadn't done the genetic manipulation.

So all that Echo and Cole and the others had speculated had happened. Every bit of it.

It was then that things really changed. Instead of having one hundred and eighty mother ships, they had closer to ten thousand to use.

So they moved mostly in one direction, seeding human galaxies as fast as they could.

Along the way the humans, Gray, and Cirrata met the Procyon, a raccoon-like race that had seeded about six galaxies. The Procyon built cities in large forests and loved the wet, damp jungles and forests around the equators of Earth-like planets.

The Procyon liked the way the humans, Gray, and Cirrata lived together on seeded planets and after a hundred thousand years or so of trade and negotiations, asked to join.

They had faster ships and other upgrades that helped everyone and they were welcomed. So from that point forward the four races all lived on and seeded the planets together.

And part of the growth of every planet was getting the races as they evolved to understand and live with the other.

As the seeding front wave neared the area of compact galaxies that they hoped to build a large center in, they discovered the Portia. They were a fist-sized spider-like race that had spread over almost fifty galaxies without ever changing a planet. They were colorful, likable, and horrific at the same time. They built small village-like cities around lakes. They hated the desert, the oceans, the mountains, and the jungles.

The images of them that Echo saw made her shudder. She had never much cared for spiders. But she had to admit their small village cities looked like fairy tale constructions of orange webs and bright blue sheets of walls that shimmered in the sunlight.

The Portia liked the other four races and were willing to trade and work with them almost from day one. Within fifty thousand years of meeting, they had joined into the seeding and were living in harmony with the other four races.

Now, almost four million years from the start, there were still over two thousand mother Seeder ships going in a hundred different directions from the massive cluster of galaxies called The Center.

Echo was impressed at the vast scale of it all and the history.

But now they were down to focusing on one human at a time. A very different, yet very important scale.

It was only a few of the humans who had decided to stay behind on each planet. All the Cirrata and Gray had left on the evacuation ships. Now, every hour, the images coming in reminded Echo of the six years she and Cole had spent helping clear out the dead and get a human society restarted on a planet in the Milky Way Galaxy. Only thankfully, this time, there were no bodies. Just people who had made a bad choice and were now willing and ready to leave.

And saving them felt great.

But something was missing. Something was starting to bother her.

She wanted to talk with Cole about it, but just as she was beginning he turned to her first and asked the question that pinpointed exactly what she was worried about.

"What are we going to do after we finish this?" he asked.

The job of rescuing survivors might take them another five to ten years. At most, before they would no longer be needed.

But during those years she desperately needed something else to focus on.

She looked up at the screen and then smiled. She knew the answer to that question. Knew it as clearly as any answer she had ever known.

"We go exploring again," she said.

Cole laughed. "Exactly what I was hoping you would say."

"Any bet that the other Starburst chairmen might feel the same way?" she asked, smiling at the man she loved more than anything.

"I would bet they all would," he said.

"So how about we have a conference call with them, suggest the idea, and get everyone planning," she said. "We only have a decade or so to get ready."

"Not a lot of time at all," he said, nodding. He pointed to the screen. "And a lot more fun than focusing on this."

Then he turned and kissed her.

She kissed him back.

"Thank you," she said.

He just smiled at her with that wonderful smile she never grew tired of, even after centuries.

Then she turned to face the big screen and all the images of ruined worlds. "*Star Trail*, please ask the other Starburst chairmen for a conference link. Tell them the topic is: *What are we going to explore next?*"

After a moment the smiling and laughing and nodding faces of the other chairmen started to push aside the images of the ruined planets.

One mission accomplished. They had found the ancients.

It was clearly time to figure out another mission for the Starburst ships.

And she had no doubt it would be fun.

If you enjoyed *Starburst*, try the next thrilling book in the
Seeders Universe series, *Rescue Two!* What follows is a sample
chapter.

PROLOGUE

The oldest man on the Seeder ship *Lost Sense* sat alone in a room.

A loud burp cut through the room.

"Sorry," he said.

He said it to no one, since he was alone in the ship and had been now for over two hundred years. He commanded, was the Chairman of, and the only passenger of, the *Lost Sense*. The ship was big enough to house fifty crew, but easy enough for one to manage, so he and the others had decided only he would risk his own life on this mission.

His name was Larry Estrabrook.

He stood six-foot-two, had dark brown hair that was still thick, and muscles in his shoulders he worked on regularly.

As a Seeder, he had lived just over four thousand years and was part of the group of humans who were long-lived and were planning to spread humanity to other galaxies, just as they had done to many planets in the First Galaxy.

He knew a couple other Seeders who were older than he was, but he still liked to think of himself as the oldest man in just about any world and on any ship in any segment of the First Galaxy.

The Seeders called themselves Seeders because of the idea of not only seeding other planets with humans, but seeding other galaxies as well. It had seemed like a great idea at the time, although Larry had no idea what loony person had come up with it.

A galaxy was damn big and it took a hundred years to just get across the spiral First Galaxy. Why did they think they could seed other planets in other galaxies?

But not only did Seeders live a long time, it seems most of them thought of big ideas as well. Like this mission he was on. He was going to be the first Seeder to travel to another galaxy.

His mission was to test a new ship, new engine, and try to make it to the nearest satellite galaxy from the First Galaxy.

When in the new galaxy, he was also supposed to scout the small cluster galaxy and look for any sign of aliens. Seeders didn't want to mess with aliens.

The small cluster galaxy he was headed for was by far the closest to home and it was still going to take a four-hundred-year trip.

And if they were depending on him to send back information about the small galaxy, it looked like they might have to wait some more years beyond his scheduled arrival.

He was stuck.

Yup, stuck.

No idea how a spaceship could get stuck in the emptiness of space between galaxies, but he had managed it.

He was supposed to be in deep sleep for most of the four-hundred-year trip, but alarm systems had rousted him about two hundred years in.

Lost Sense was basically dead in a weird area of space. He couldn't see anything past the edge of whatever he had run into. His deep-space drive didn't work even though it was still in top condition, so he was going to have to use his sub-light-system drives to push himself out of whatever he was stuck in.

And that was going to take time.

At this point he had been working to get out for almost two years and maybe in another year he would reach the edge.

He almost thought about going back into cold sleep, but decided he needed to stay awake and pay attention for the years this would take.

Seemed like a good idea two boring years ago.

Not so much now.

He was working on some calculations and just happened to be sitting in his command chair in the three-person command center when things changed on the big screen in front of his chair.

There were thousands of small flashes of light along the surface of what seemed to be inside. And then, where a moment before it had shown a blank sort of nothingness, now the stars were back.

Lost Sense was back in regular space.

He jumped from his chair with both hands in the air and shouted "Yes!" Then he quickly went back to his instruments.

All his ship's systems were working.

Oh, wow, now he could have a good steak dinner, a glass of wine, and get back to sleep to complete his mission.

Only one big problem.

Nothing about space around him looked right.

Nothing at all.

At this point the small cluster galaxy should be filling space ahead of him, but there was nothing there.

The big spiral First Galaxy was farther away from him than he had lifetimes to return to, even if he was the oldest man alive.

None of this was possible.

None of it.

"Chairman Estrabrook?" a voice asked over his unused communications system.

Larry jerked. Looked around at the empty command center, then just sat back and laughed. He must still be in deep sleep and all of this was a malfunctioning sleep chamber causing him to dream. No one could be talking to him out here in literally the middle of nothingness.

"This is Chairman Evan West of the Seeder ship *Rescue Two*. Welcome back."

"Did I go somewhere?" Larry asked, wondering why this dream even had names in it.

At that point a ship so large it blocked out most of the stars on one side of his big screen flashed into existence and stopped.

He tried to get an image of the ship, but it was so large he failed.

He felt like a guppy next to a whale. He could tell that the new ship was in the shape of a bird of prey. He had heard rumors that the Seeders were going to design their ships like that, but it hadn't started when he left.

In two hundred years they had made a lot of progress, or something was really, really wrong.

"You were trapped in a Void Space Bubble," Chairman West said. "Time and space do not work the same inside of one of those, so we popped the bubble to get you out."

"Okay," Larry said, starting to feel a little panicked and starting to realize his mission was most likely over.

"With your permission, we would like to take your ship into our docking bay and get you to a Seeder Base. There are a lot of people who are excited to meet and talk with you."

"Why?" Larry asked.

"Because of how old you are," Chairman West said. "You have knowledge about the early days of the Seeders that has been long forgotten."

"How much time has passed?" Larry asked, not really wanting to know the answer, but it was starting to seem that if this was not a dream, he was going to have to face the answer.

"Just over seven million years," Chairman West said.

Again, Larry just laughed.

No way he could even begin to grasp seven million years.

But that explained the galaxies not being where they were supposed to be.

"And it was some of your friends who were also trapped in Void Space Bubbles that suggested we go looking for you."

"I have seven-million-year-old friends?" Larry asked.

"They were trapped for millions of years, just as you have been. Many of them always wondered what happened to you. So they told us, as best they could, what path you took and we found you."

"Thank you," Larry said.

He would have to ask later exactly what it took to find him and rescue him.

"Chairman Ray would like to talk with you for a few minutes," Chairman West said. "He is sort of the person who runs all the Seeders and has now for millions of years. Would that be all right? We'll bring you aboard and get your ship on our hanger deck. With your permission."

Larry just laughed. "Seems like I have no choice. Even at full speed, it would take me another million years to get back to the First Galaxy. How long will it take with you?"

"Five minutes," Chairman West said.

Larry once more laughed until he realized Chairman West was perfectly serious.

Larry took a deep breath and looked around. Nothing holding him here.

"Sure, I would be glad to talk with Chairman Ray and catch a ride home."

"Great," Chairman West said.

A moment later, with no feeling at all of movement, Larry found himself standing in an ultra-modern, yet surprisingly comfortable conference room with a long table and eight chairs, facing a man about Larry's height with a large smile on his face.

"It is an honor to meet you," Chairman West said, stepping forward and shaking Larry's hand.

"I think the honor is all mine," Larry said.

At that moment a man appeared next to Chairman West. He had long gray hair, perfectly straight that ran down his back, and wore slacks and a dress shirt that looked like it was right out of Larry's time.

Actually Chairman West wore about the same thing, so looked like fashions for Seeders hadn't changed much.

"I am Chairman Ray," the man said and stepped forward with his hand outstretched. "It is an honor to meet you, Chairman Estrabrook."

"Why is it an honor to meet me?" Larry asked. "You rescued me, from what I am starting to understand. This should be all my honor."

Chairman Ray smiled and nodded to West who brought up an image on the screen. It was of the First Galaxy and the surrounding smaller galaxies that orbited the First Galaxy.

"When you left on your mission," Ray said, "the First Galaxy was about half seeded with human planets."

Larry nodded to that.

"Where you were headed is now called The Misty Galaxy. When you were lost, your name became lore and a warning of the dangers of moving between galaxies in deep space. You were considered a hero."

"Well, I slept for two hundred years until I got stuck," Larry said. "I suppose that's heroic."

Chairman Ray ignored him and just went on. "Then a few thousand years after you were lost, one of the first of what we call Mother Seeder Ships with over four million souls on board, headed toward the Misty Galaxy. It also vanished without a trace into a different Void Space Bubble."

"We just found that ship last year," West said. "And it was many on board that ship that suggested we search for you. We will be taking you to the same base where most of them are at now."

Larry just nodded and said, "Thanks."

"Now let me show you what has happened since you have been gone," Ray said. "And what you started."

"All five of the satellite galaxies around the First Galaxy were seeded finally," West said.

The image on the screen pulled back to show all of them colored in a soft gold color.

"Then we moved out," Ray said, "and we ended up seeding almost one thousand galaxies at this point and are still expanding."

Larry again just laughed as the image pulled way back showing the orange points of light that represented full galaxies with billions and billions of stars in each one.

"There are millions and millions of human planets in each one of those lights," West said.

"A new Seeder Mother ship is now coming online every few weeks," Ray said, "and we are finishing the seeding of a new galaxy now about every three months."

Larry just moved over to a chair and sat down, shaking his head. He just felt tired and totally overwhelmed.

"We'll be docking in the *SunWorld Seeder Base* in a minute," West said.

"Where is my place in all of that now?" Larry asked, indicating the screen.

"Spend a few years learning what is happening now," Ray said, "see what is even possible, talk with some of your old friends, get used to being so far into your future."

"Is this possible to get used to?" Larry asked.

West laughed. "It is. And if you need help, we have it for you. Millions are going through what you are experiencing right now because once we discovered Void Space Bubbles and how to rescue those stuck inside them, we have been doing so regularly."

"And we hope you will spend some time with some of the Seeder historians," Ray said. "Help them fill in some holes in history."

Larry just laughed. "You mean my former world."

"Exactly," Ray said. "But isn't that the way it is for all of us as we age through all of our lives? Our worlds become former worlds. And those former worlds become history."

"Got that right," Larry said. "For some of us just a little quicker than others."

Both Ray and West had to agree to that.

NEWSLETTER SIGN-UP

Follow Dean on BookBub

Be the first to know!

Just sign up for the Dean Wesley Smith newsletter, and keep up
with the latest news, releases and so much more—even the
occasional giveaway.
So, what are you waiting for? To sign up go to
deanwesleysmith.com.

But wait! There's more. Sign up for the WMG Publishing
newsletter, too, and get the latest news and releases from all of
the WMG authors and lines, including Kristine Kathryn Rusch,
Kristine Grayson, Kris Nelscott, *Pulphouse Fiction Magazine*,
Smith's Monthly, and so much more.
To sign up go to wmgpublishing.com.

ABOUT THE AUTHOR

Considered one of the most prolific writers working in modern fiction, *USA Today* bestselling writer Dean Wesley Smith published far more than a hundred novels in forty years, and hundreds of short stories across many genres.

At the moment he produces novels in several major series, including the time travel Thunder Mountain novels set in the Old West, the galaxy-spanning Seeders Universe series, the urban fantasy Ghost of a Chance series, a superhero series starring Poker Boy, and a mystery series featuring the retired detectives of the Cold Poker Gang.

His monthly magazine, *Smith's Monthly*, which consists of only his own fiction, premiered in October 2013 and offers readers more than 70,000 words per issue, including a new and original novel every month.

During his career, Dean also wrote a couple dozen *Star Trek* novels, the only two original *Men in Black* novels, Spider-Man and X-Men novels, plus novels set in gaming and television worlds. Writing with his wife Kristine Kathryn Rusch under the name Kathryn Wesley, he wrote the novel for the NBC miniseries The Tenth Kingdom and other books for *Hallmark Hall of Fame* movies.

He wrote novels under dozens of pen names in the worlds

of comic books and movies, including novelizations of almost a dozen films, from *The Final Fantasy* to *Steel* to *Rundown.*

Dean also worked as a fiction editor off and on, starting at Pulphouse Publishing, then at *VB Tech Journal*, then Pocket Books, and now at WMG Publishing, where he and Kristine Kathryn Rusch serve as series editors for the acclaimed *Fiction River* anthology series.

For more information about Dean's books and ongoing projects, please visit his website at www.deanwesleysmith.com and sign up for his newsletter.

For more information:
www.deanwesleysmith.com

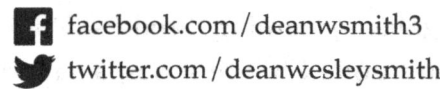 facebook.com/deanwsmith3
twitter.com/deanwesleysmith